The
BOY
DISCARD
who
SWAM WITH
PIRANHAS

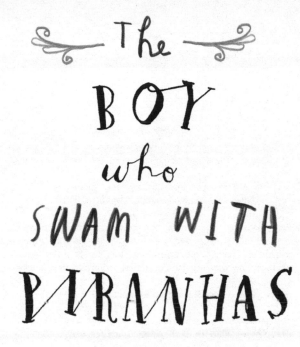

The
BOY
who
SWAM WITH
PIRANHAS

DAVID ALMOND

illustrated by

OLIVER JEFFERS

CANDLEWICK PRESS

Text copyright © 2012 by David Almond
Illustrations copyright © 2012 by Oliver Jeffers

First U.S. paperback edition 2015

Library of Congress Catalog Card Number 2012947721
ISBN 978-0-7636-6169-4 (hardcover)
ISBN 978-0-7636-7680-3 (paperback)

14 15 16 17 18 19 BVG 10 9 8 7 6 5 4 3 2 1

Printed in Berryville, VA, U.S.A.

This book was typeset in Rockwell.
The illustrations were done in mixed media.

Candlewick Press
99 Dover Street
Somerville, Massachusetts 02144

visit us at www.candlewick.com

For Hella
D. A.

Here's a question. How would you like it if somebody in your house—your uncle Ernie, for instance—decided to turn it into a fish-canning factory? How would you like it if there were buckets of pilchards and tubs of mackerel everywhere you looked? What if a shoal of sardines was swimming in the bath? What if your uncle Ernie kept on making more and more machines—machines for chopping the heads off, cutting the tails off, getting the guts out; machines for cleaning them and boiling them and squashing them into cans? Can you imagine the racket? Can you picture the mess? And just think about the stink!

What if your uncle Ernie's machines grew so big that they took over every room—your bedroom, for instance, so that you had to sleep in a cupboard? What if your uncle Ernie said you couldn't go to school anymore but had to stay at home to help him can the fish? Sounds good? Ah, but what if instead of going to school you had to start work every morning at six o'clock on the dot? And you got no holidays? And you never saw your old pals? Would you like that? Would you heck! Well, neither did Stanley Potts.

Stanley Potts. Just an ordinary kid living an ordinary life in an ordinary house in an ordinary street. Then, bang! Life turned barmy. It happened overnight. One day, there they were—Stan, his uncle Ernie and his auntie Annie—living in a lovely little terraced house in Fish Quay Lane. Next day, wallop! Pilchards, mackerel, sardines, and total barminess.

Now, Stan really did love his uncle Ernie and his auntie Annie. Ernie was Stan's dad's brother. They'd been wonderful to him, ever since Stan's dad died in that awful accident and his mum died of a broken heart. They'd been like a brand-new mum and dad. But once the barminess started, it seemed it would never stop. And pretty soon it would all get far too much to bear.

1.

THE FACTORY

ONE

It all started when Simpson's Shipyard shut.
Simpson's had been on the river since the year
dot. Blokes that lived by the river had been working at Simpson's since the year dot. Stan's dad
had worked there until the accident. Uncle Ernie
had worked there since he was a lad, just like his
brother and their dad and their dad's dad and
their dad's dad's dad. Then—*kapow!*—it was all
over. They made cheaper ships and better ships
in Korea and Taiwan and China and Japan. So
Simpson's gates were slammed shut and the work-
ers were given a few quid each and told to go away
and the demolition gangs moved in. No more jobs
for blokes like Uncle Ernie. But blokes like Uncle
Ernie were proud and hard-working and they had
families to care for.

Some found other jobs—in Perkins' Plastic
Packaging Factory, for instance, or answering
telephones for the Common Benefit Insurance and
Financial Society or filling shelves at Stuffco or
showing folks round the Great Industrial Heritage

Museum (special exhibits: Superb Ships Shaped at Simpson's Shipyard Since the Year Dot). Some blokes just turned glum and shuffled round the streets all day or hung about on street corners or got ill and started to fade away. A few turned to the bottle, a few turned to crime, and a couple ended up in the clink. But some, like Stan's uncle, Mr. Ernest Potts, had big, big plans.

A couple of months after they'd flung him out of Simpson's, Ernie was standing with Stan and Annie on the riverbank. The cranes and the warehouses were being torn down. Fences and walls were getting smashed. There was wreckage all around. Wharves and jetties were being ripped apart. The air was filled with the noise of wrenching and ripping and banging and smashing. The earth trembled and juddered under their feet. The river was all wild waves and turbulence. The wind whipped in from the distant sea. Seagulls screeched like they'd never seen anything like it.

Ernie had been yelling and groaning and moaning for weeks. Now he sighed and grunted and cursed and spat.

"The world's gone mad!" he yelled into the

wind. "It's gone absolutely bonkers!" He stamped his feet. He shook his fists at the sky. "But you'll not beat me!" he yelled. "No, you'll not get the better of Ernest Potts!"

And he looked beyond the old shipyard to where the river opened out to the shimmering silvery sea. There was a trawler coming in. It was red and beautiful and there was a flock of white seagulls all around it. It was lovely, shining in the sunlight and bouncing on the tide. It was a vision. It was like something arriving from a dream. It was a gift, a gorgeous promise. The trawler came to rest at the fish quay. A massive netful of beautiful silvery fish was unloaded. Ernie looked at the fish, and suddenly everything became plain to him.

"That's the answer!" he cried.

"What's the answer?" said Annie.

"What's the question?" said Stan.

But too late. Ernie was off. He belted down to the quay and bought a couple of pounds of pilchards. He belted home and put the pilchards on to boil. He got his wheelbarrow and he belted back to Annie and Stan, who were still standing there on the riverbank. He put a few sheets of scrap metal onto the barrow.

Annie and Stan trotted at his side as he wobbled back home with them.

"What you doing, Ernie?" asked Annie.

"What you doing, Uncle Ernie?" asked Stan.

Ernie just winked at them. He dumped the metal in the garden. He opened his toolbox and took out his cutting gear and his welding gear and his pliers and his hammers, and he set to work cutting the sheets of metal and welding and hammering them into cylinders and curves.

"What you doing, Ernie?" asked Annie again.

"What you doing, Uncle Ernie?" asked Stan again.

Ernie pushed back his welding visor. He grinned. He winked. "Changing the world!" he said. He snapped the visor shut again.

Half an hour later, he'd made his first can. It was heavy and lumpy and rusty and misshapen but it was a can. Half an hour after

that, the boiled and pulpy pilchards were squashed into it and a lid was welded on it.

Ernie scribbled the name onto the can with a felt tip: **Potts's Pilchards.**

He punched the air. He did a little dance. "It works!" he declared.

Annie and Stan inspected the can. They looked into Ernie's goggly eyes. Ernie's eyes goggled back at them.

"There's a long way to go," said Ernie, "but it absolutely, positively, definitely works."

He cleared his throat. "The future of this family," he announced, "will be in the fish-canning business!"

And that was the start of Ernie's great venture: Potts's Spectacular Sardines; Potts's Magnificent Mackerel; and Potts's Perfect Potted Pilchards.

TWo

Ernie welded and hammered and nailed and drilled and screwed. He lifted floors and knocked down walls. He built a network of pipes and tubes and sluices and drains. He connected wires and switches and fuse boards. His machines grew and grew and grew and grew until they were in every corridor and every room. Pipes and cables ran under every floor and through every wall. The house throbbed with the beat of engines, with the snip and snap of guillotines and knives, with the whiz and whirr of electric saws, with the gush of sluicing water, with the bubbling of great cauldrons. And with Ernie's excited cries.

"Work faster! Work harder! Oh, my wonderful machines! Oh, how I love them! Fish, fish, fish, FISH! Machine, machine, machine, MACHINE!"

Every morning, trucks brought buckets of fish to the front door. Every evening, trucks picked up crates of tinned fish from the back. Business boomed. Money poured in. Ernie wasn't a struggling ex–shipyard worker now. He was a businessman, an entrepreneur. His empire grew like it was a living thing.

Every night, Stan slept in his cupboard and Ernie and Annie slept under a huge gutting machine.

The next morning at six o'clock, the alarm clock would ring.

RING-A-DING-A-DING-A-DING-A-DING-A-DING!

And straight away a hooter hooted:

NEE-NAW-NEE-NAW-NEE-NAW-NEE-NAW!

And straight away a record played:

WAKEY-WAKEY! WAKEY-WAKEY!

And straight away Ernie yelled:

"UP! COME ON, YOU LOT! UP! SIX O'CLOCK AND TIME TO START! GET TO WORK!"

When Annie groaned or Stan moaned, Ernie's response would be the same:

"THIS IS FOR US! FOR THIS FAMILY! NOW COME ON! IT'S SIX O'CLOCK AND TIME TO START!"

But one morning, Annie said, "Hold on, Ernie."

"What do you mean, 'Hold on, Ernie'?"

"I mean slow down. Just for today."

Ernie was already in action. He had his gutting

gloves on. He held his snipping scissors and he jangled his keys, and fish swam and danced and slithered through his brain.

"Ernie!" yelled Annie. "Slow down just for today!"

"What's so blooming special about today?"

"You don't remember, do you?" said Annie.

"Remember what?"

She took an envelope from under her pillow and waved it at him. "Do you not remember? It's Stan's *birthday.*"

"Is it?" said Ernie. "Ah, aye! Of course it is. Today is Stan's birthday." He shrugged. "So what?"

"So let's be nice to him. Let's do birthday things."

"Birthday things?" He frowned. "What d'you mean, birthday things?"

"I mean presents and parties and smiles and singing 'Happy Birthday' and . . . not bothering him with potty pilchards for one thing!"

"*Potty* pilchards? I'll have you know that pilchards is our lifeblood, madam! I'll have you know that—"

"And I'll have *you* know that if you're not nice to your nephew today, your wife will be on strike!"

Ernie flinched.

"Now hush," said Annie. She got up and tiptoed to Stan's cupboard. "Morning, son," she whispered.

Stan grabbed his work clothes. "Sorry!" he said. "Am I late? Should I be up? Is it time to start?"

But Annie hugged him. "Happy birthday, Stan!" she said.

The lad was astonished. "What?" he said. "It's my birthday?"

"Of course," replied Annie. "Didn't you know?"

Stan pondered. "I remember thinking it *might* be. . . . But nobody said anything, so I thought I must be wrong. Or that you must have forgotten."

"Ah, Stan," said Annie. "Do you think we'd forget something like that? We remembered all along. Didn't we, Ernie?"

Ernie coughed. He snipped the air with his scissors. "Course we did," he said. He tried to grin through the cupboard doorway. "Happy birthday, lad! Happy, happy, happy, birthday! Ha, ha, ha, ha, ha, ha, ha, ha! Go on. Give him the card, then."

Annie gave Stan the envelope. Stan took out the card. There was a picture of a sailing ship on it and a message inside.

"Oh, thank you!" cried
Stan. "Thank you. It's the
best card ever!"

"Right!" said Ernie.
"That's quite enough
of that. There's fish to
be canned!" And
he turned back to
his buckets of fish
and his magnificent machines.

"What a silly!" said Annie. "Why don't we let
him get on with his fish while we have a lovely
breakfast?"

She opened a carrier bag and took out some
cans of pop and some chocolate bars and a big
bag of sweets. They giggled and tucked in. Every
few minutes, Ernie yelled, **"WHERE ARE YOU?
YOU'RE LATE! STOP SLACKING! GET TO
WORK!"**

But Annie just said, "Take no notice." And when
they'd finished all the pop and all the chocolate
and all the sweets, she said, "Now, Stan. You're
going to have a treat today. Just you wait there."

THRee

Ernie was pressing buttons and flicking switches and pulling levers and twisting knobs. He jerked and swayed and danced and whirled. He chanted his fish chants and sang his fish songs at the top of his voice.

"Fish fish fish fish
FISH FISH FISH FISH!
Fish in buckets and fish in bins,
Chop off their heads and tails and fins!
Boil and sizzle with tomato sauce
And slap them in a tin, with a label, of course!
Fish fish fish fish
FISH FISH FISH FISH!
Potts's Perfect Pilchards! Spectacular Sardines!
Magnificent Mackerel! Elegant Eels!
Haddock and herring and cod and squid!
Get them down your neck—best thing you ever did!
Fish fish fish fish
FISH FISH FISH FISH!
Fish in buckets and . . ."

Annie sighed. Whatever had happened to the nice easy-going feller she used to know? She tapped him on the shoulder. No response. She thumped him on the back. No response. She walloped him and yelled into his ear, "Ernie! ERNEST POTTS!"

He turned to her at last. "Aha! About time!" he said. "STAN! Where are you, lad?"

Annie reached down and switched off the nearest machine. Ernie gasped. What on earth was she doing? He reached down to switch it back on, when Annie said, "Never mind Stan. It's his day off."

"Day off? Says *who*?"

"Says *me*," said Annie. "It's a new rule. Look, I've written it down." She handed him a slip of paper.

RULE 1.
FAMily mEmbers gET a DAY OFF
on their BIRTHDAY

Ernie read it and scratched his head.

"You had rules in the shipyard, didn't you?" asked Annie.

"Yes," said Ernie, "but—"

"No buts," said Annie. "And he also gets a ten-pound bonus." She handed him another slip of paper.

> RULE 1a.
>
> FAMILY MEMBERS get a £10 bonus on THEIR BIRTHDAY

"But you've just made these rules up!" Ernie exclaimed.

Annie shrugged. "Course I have. Are you objecting?" She looked Ernie in the eye.

He looked Annie in the eye. "Yes!" he said.

She handed him another slip of paper.

> RULE 1b.
>
> Don't you dare object or I will go ON STRIKE

"Well?" Annie said.

Ernie grunted. He reached into his pocket. He drew out a ten-pound note.

"Give it to Stan and tell him to have a good time,"

ordered Annie. She raised a finger as if to say,
Don't you dare object! "Stan!" she called. "Come
here, son. Uncle Ernie has something to tell you."

Stan came out of the cupboard.

"You've got a day off," said Annie. "Isn't that
right, love?"

"Aye!" grunted Ernie.

"And Ernie's got something for you, haven't you,
Ernie?"

"Aye!" grunted Ernie again. He held out the
ten-pound note. "Happy birthday, son," he said.
"Have a . . ." He scratched his head. What were
the words he was supposed to say?

"A good time!" prompted Annie.

"That's it," said Ernie. "Have a
good time, lad."

"Where will I have a good
time?" asked Stan.

Annie opened the front door.
"Out there," she said. "You've
been cooped up too long in here.
Have a good time out there in the
world, son!"

Annie and Stan looked out

through the streets, and they gasped in wonder and surprise. Because a fairground had come to town. There it was, slap bang in the place where Simpson's Shipyard used to be. There was the Ferris wheel turning slowly in the sun. And the pointed top of a helter-skelter. The crackle of dodgems, the wail of music, the clatter of a roller coaster. There was the smell of engine oil and candyfloss and hot dogs.

"A fair!" they said together. "Wow!"

Stan gripped his ten pounds tight, and he kissed his aunt and grinned at his uncle and stepped out into his sunny day of freedom.

Annie grabbed a shopping bag. "Rule one c," she said as she walked out. "Aunts are allowed time off to buy birthday cakes!"

Ernie watched them go. "The world's gone barmy," he said to himself, then he slammed the door and got back to work.

FOUR

Down went Stan through the terraced streets, past the Shipwright's Arms and the Salvation Army hostel and the Oxfam shop and the shuffling men. He ran across the waste ground to the fair. It was huge and noisy and bright, and the merry-go-rounds were turning, but it was still early, so hardly anybody was there. Just a handful of truants, a couple of women pushing ancient buggies, more glum-looking shuffling men, and the fairground folk themselves, with gold teeth and shocks of hair, silver studs glinting in their cheeks and bags of chinking coins around their waists. They leaned on their rides and their stalls, swigged mugs of tea and smoked strange-smelling cigarettes. They stared at Stan as he stepped shyly by. They muttered together in strange accents. They coughed and cursed and spat and roared with laughter.

Stan rode a merry-go-round all alone and he spun on the waltzer all alone. All alone he rose into the air on the Ferris wheel. He looked down on his world: the river, the terraced streets, the spaces where all the shipyards and the factories used to be. He saw his old school, St. Mungo's, and all the kids playing in the playground. He saw his own home in Fish Quay Lane. He saw the steam from his uncle's machines seething through its roof. Round he went, up and down, round and round and up and down. He saw the distant city and the distant mountains. He saw the glittering lovely sea going on forever, the deep blue lovely sky going on forever. He remembered his lovely mum and dad, and high up there in the sky he shed a few quiet tears for them. He thought of his aunt and uncle and he gave thanks for them. He imagined the world beyond the sea and the universe beyond the sky, and his head reeled at the vastness of it all and the astonishingness of it all.

Down at earth again, he ate a slithery hot dog and sticky candyfloss. He licked his lips and his fingers and wandered past an ancient red and green Gypsy caravan. **GYPSY ROSE** was painted above its little doorway. A white pony stood beside it, wearing a nosebag. A woman in a brightly patterned shawl came to the door. She beckoned Stan with her forefinger.

"I am the great-great-granddaughter of the true Gypsy Rose," she told him. "Come inside and cross my palm with silver. I will fill your head with wonders and secrets in return."

Stan licked the last of the candyfloss from his fingers.

"I will tell you when your time of troubles will be at an end," Gypsy Rose said.

"How d'you know I've got troubles?" said Stan.

"It's clear to them with eyes to see. What is your name, young man?"

"Stan," said Stan.

"Give me just a single piece of silver, Stan," she said. She lowered her voice. "Be brave and come inside."

Stan was about to step up into the caravan when his eye was caught by a flickering of gold.

Goldfish. They were hanging in a line on a hook-a-duck stall. There were thirteen of them, tiny goldfish, each one swimming in a tiny plastic bag that dangled on an orange string and hung there in the sun. Without thinking, he moved away from Gypsy Rose towards the fish.

Gypsy Rose spoke again. "Farewell," she said.

"You are entranced. You will be dejected. You will travel. And we will meet again."

She went back inside. Stan moved closer to the hook-a-duck stall. The bags were so tiny, the amounts of water so small; the fish were so lovely, so miraculous, with their golden skin and their gills and their fins and their panting mouths and their delicate scales and their tender dark eyes. He reached up towards one.

"Oi! Wotya doin', kid?"

Stan flinched. A man appeared, standing inside the stall below the fish.

"I said wotya doin'?"

Stan shook his head. "Just looking at the fish," he whispered.

The man was little with a shiny smooth face and black hair that came to a pointy widow's peak. He had a single golden earring. He wore ancient,

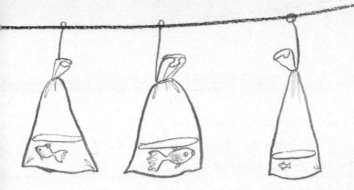

dusty red satin with splashes of grease on it. Behind him, dirty plastic ducks with hooks on their heads floated in endless circles on a green plastic pool. Beyond the ducks was an old caravan. A girl stared gloomily out from its murky window. She rubbed the glass with her fingertip and made a tiny peephole and peeped through it at Stan.

"No jus' lookin'!" snapped the man. "You got to win them, boy."

He pointed to a sign:

HOOK - a - DUCK
EZ a GO
A PRIZE EV'RY TIME

Stan looked at his money: less than two pounds left, not even enough for a single turn.

"But it's cruel!" he protested. "They've got hardly any water and they—"

The man just shrugged. "You want to help them, you got to win them," he said. He looked past Stan into the fair.

Stan saw that the tiniest goldfish of all was hardly moving, was coming to a halt. "But they're dying!" he said.

The man glanced at the fish, then shrugged again. "They die, I get some more," he said. "S'easy."

"But I could save them!"

"How much ye got?" asked the man.

"One pound sixty-six," said Stan.

The man pointed to the sign: £2 A GO.

"But what good is it if it's dead?" begged Stan. He held out his £1.66. "Please, mister! Please!"

The man sniffed. He looked at the money on Stan's palm.

"OK," he sighed. "Call me a softie. But ye got to take the dyin' one. And no cheatin'!"

He took the money and gave Stan a long stick with a dangling string and a hook on the end. Stan reached towards the cruising ducks, but he was shaking and trembling, and he couldn't stop looking up at the dying fish in its tiny bag of water.

The man clicked his tongue. "Kids these days!" he muttered. "Don't nobody even teach ye to hook proper?"

And he slipped Stan's hook onto a duck and Stan lifted it from the water. He grabbed the bag with the dying fish in it. But he just couldn't leave the others.

"They'll all die!" he said. "If nobody wins them, they'll . . ."

The man held out his palm.

"But I've got nothing left!"

The man contemplated Stan. "Ye could work for them, I s'pose," he said.

"Work?" said Stan.

"Aye," said the man. He nodded to himself. "That's a good idea. If, that is, ye know what work is."

"I do know!" said Stan.

"Huh! That'll make a change." The man stroked his chin. "Ye could, fer instance, scrub them ducks." He spat on the ground. "Jus' look at the state of them. They're filthy."

"OK," said Stan quickly. He rolled up his sleeves. "What do I do?"

The man pointed at a plastic bucket. "Ye get

23

that scrubber and ye get that soap and ye scrub. S'dead easy."

Stan got straight to it. He scrubbed the ducks frantically. He kept glancing up at the fish. They turned slowly and more slowly in their little plastic bags.

"That's very good that," said the man. "Me daughter's s'posed to do it but she thinks it's beneath her. That's her back there, look, the big lazy lump."

Stan stole a quick glance. The pale girl peeped through her peephole.

"She's called Nitasha," said the man. He looked at her and shook his head, then pointed at Stan, who worked faster and faster till all the ducks were shining bright. Nitasha turned up her nose and looked away.

The man began to pick up the ducks and inspect them.

"Can I have the fish now?" pleaded Stan.

The man held up a small yellow duck. "Little dab of muck left here," he said.

Stan grabbed it, scrubbed it, polished it again.

"Now?" said Stan.

The man pondered. He slowly lifted an orange duck to his eyes. Stan couldn't bear it. By now all the fish were floundering, were drifting, weren't swimming, were dropping slowly downwards in their little plastic bags.

"I'll have them now!" he said. "They're mine!" And he stretched up and took all twelve of them down, hanging the bags from his outstretched fingers. "OK?" he demanded.

"What's yer name?" said the man.

But Stan was already running towards the river. He ran out of the fair and across the rubble and past the derelict sheds and warehouses and slithered through an ancient iron fence and flung himself down onto the edge of the riverbank, where there was just a short drop to the water,

and he lowered the plastic bags one by one and allowed the river water to fill them up. Then he held them up to the sky. The water in the bags was murkier now. Little bits and fragments swirled in it and greasy slicks floated at the top. But in each one of them, at the centre of the murk, there was a flicker and flash of living gold.

Stan sighed with relief and delight. Then he noticed the man from the stall, standing close behind him.

"Ye're a softie, aren't you?" said the man. "But I can see ye're a good worker. What's yer name?"

"Stan," said Stan.

"I'm Dostoyevsky," said the man. He stretched out his hand. Stan didn't take it. Dostoyevsky shrugged. "I ain't so bad as I seem," he said. "How d'ye fancy a job on the hook-a-duck stall?"

"No, thank you, Mr. Dostoyevsky," said Stan.

"I'd pay ye well," said Dostoyevsky. "It's steady work. Whatever problems come into the world, there'll always be a need fer the hook-a-duck stall."

But Stan said no again, and headed homeward with the thirteen goldfish dangling from his fingers.

Five

Back at 69 Fish Quay Lane, there'd been Trouble.

While Stan was at the hook-a-duck stall, a rusty white van pulled up outside the house. It had massive writing on it:

DAFT

DEPARTMINT For the ABOLISHUN of Fishy Things
www.DAFT.gov

sumthing fishy going on?
WANt to get sumbody into TRUBLe?
CALL the Snitch-on-a-naybor line
0191 876 5432

ALL CALLS TREATED in STRICTEST CONFIDANCE

There was a tiny window in the side of the van. Behind the window, there was a telescope pointing straight at Ernie's house. Behind the telescope, there was a little man.

"Just what we thunk," muttered the man to himself. "How disgracious. How absolutely appallin'."

He scribbled notes into a notepad. He straightened his shirt. He fastened his black tie neatly. He wedged a black leather folder under his arm. Then he stepped out of the van and rapped on Ernie's door.

Ernie, of course, with all the banging and clanging and chanting and singing, heard nothing. The man rapped again. Again, no answer. He leaned down and peered through the letter box.

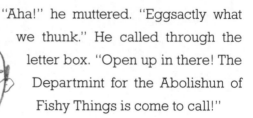

"Aha!" he muttered. "Eggsactly what we thunk." He called through the letter box. "Open up in there! The Departmint for the Abolishun of Fishy Things is come to call!"

No answer.

He yelled again.

No answer.

He tutted and grunted and stamped his feet. "How disgracious. How absolutely appallin'." He grabbed the door handle. "I is now coming in!" he called.

The door opened easily. The man stepped inside. He was confronted by pipes, by cables, by whirring wheels and spinning cogs, by buckets of fish and boxes of tins. He stepped forward, investigating as he went. He scribbled in his notepad.

"How absolutely disgustin'," he said. "What a nutter disgrace!"

He heard Ernie singing. He saw Ernie sprawled across a machine, kicking a lever with his left foot, spinning a cog with his right, clicking a switch with his right hand, pressing a button with his left.

"Machine!" yelled Ernie. "Machine, machine, machine, machine!"

"Ahem," said the investigator. "AHEM!"

Ernie looked round. "Who the heck are you?" he said.

The investigator clicked his heels. "I is," he said, "a DAFT envistigator."

"A *what*?" said Ernie.

"A envistigator," said the investigator. "A envistigator what envistigates things. *Strange* things. *Peculiar* things. Things what shouldn't even *be* things." He stepped a little closer. "*Fishy* things!"

He narrowed his eyes. "And there's something fishy here, Mr. . . ." He raised his pencil, ready to note Ernie's name.

"Mr. None Of Your Business," said Ernie. He broke free of his levers and switches. "Mr. Get Out Of My Blooming House!" he said. "Mr. Who Do You Think You Are Coming In Here Without A By Your Leave! Mr. If You Don't Shift Your Bum I Might Just Have To Kick It! Mr. —"

The investigator raised his hand. "Not a very entilligent approach," he said. "You is talking to Mr. Clarence P. Clapp, Esquire, trained envistigator first grade, with seven stars, two pips, and a certificate signed by none other than His Grand Fishiness, the Departmint Leader hisself. Touch me and you is in deep, deep trouble, Mr. . . ."

Ernie clamped his lips tight shut.

"Ha!" said Clarence P. Clapp. "The tight-lipped method. The silent approach. I has been taught everything there is to know about that method, and let me tell you it will get you eggsactly nowhere!" He cast a beady eye around the house. "This," he said, "is not allowed. Nor is this and nor is this and nor is this and nor is this. And *this* is absolutely disgracious and *that* is absolutely appallin' and this thing here is the worst thing that I has ever, ever *saw.*" He scribbled a little more. He pursed his lips and narrowed his eyes. "What eggsactly has been going on in here, Mr. Silent?"

"Nothing!" said Ernie.

Clarence scribbled down his reply. "And," he continued, "how long eggsactly has it been going on?"

"Never!" said Ernie.

"Ha!" declared Clarence. "These answers I know is nothing but atishoo of lies! My training has prepared me for everything! I see what a disgracious state of affairs exists here, and it cannot go on and it will be stopped!"

"Oh, yeah?" said Ernie.

"Oh, yeah!" said Clarence P. Clapp. "I has the letter of the law on my side. I has the power vested in me by the High Chief Envistigator of Fishy Things. I will write my report and a notice will be served and all this will come to a nutter and absolute stop! I leave you my card." He shoved a business card into Ernie's hand. Then he turned and headed back towards the front door.

He paused for a moment. "If I was you, Mr. Silent," he said softly, "I would set to work right now this very minute to get this house back to normal or the departmint will be coming down on you like a ton of bricks! Farewell! Or should I say, *vasta la hista*!"

And out he went, slamming the door behind him.

SIX

Stan ran back across the waste ground, through the terraced streets, and up Fish Quay Lane towards home. The DAFT van passed by but he didn't notice it. He was entranced by his fish, obsessed by his fish. He slipped in through the door and went to find an empty bucket. Then he filled it full of lovely clear water and slipped his lovely goldfish into it one by one. There they were, thirteen beautiful, miraculous creatures, swimming together and free before his eyes.

His uncle was already back at work. The machines were booming and banging and clashing louder than ever. Ernie was yelling louder than ever.

Stan lifted the bucket of fish. "Don't worry about the noise," he whispered to them. "It's just my uncle Ernie. I'll look after you forever and ever and ever."

"STAN! STAN! GET HERE, LAD!"

Stan turned. "But, Uncle Ernie—" he started.

"NEVER MIND 'BUT UNCLE ERNIE'! GET HERE, LAD!"

Ernie waved him forward. "There's a crisis!" he said. "A blooming great huge massive catastrophe!"

Stan shuffled slowly towards him. "But, Uncle Ernie—" he said.

"We're under attack and all you can say is 'But Uncle Ernie'! Get here! Pull that lever, switch that switch, grease that blinking engine!" He caught sight of the fish. "What's *them*?"

Stan realized he was still carrying the bucket. "They're goldfish," he said. "I won them at the fair. I won that little one with your birthday money, Uncle Ernie."

Ernie curled his lip. "Huh!" he said. "Scrawny little things!"

"But look," said Stan. He held them towards his uncle, so that he could see their loveliness for himself.

Ernie squinted at them, then dipped his finger into the water.

"Goldfish!" he grunted at last. "What good's goldfish to a man like me. Pilchards is the fish that matter. Pilchards and haddock

and cod and . . ." He lowered his hand further into the water and the goldfish swam around it.

"See?" said Stan. "Aren't they just lovely?"

Ernie gazed down, pondering. He felt the fins and tails of the little fish as they flickered past his fingers.

"Thanks for the ten pounds, Uncle Ernie," said Stan. Then he said a thing that he'd regret for ever after. "If you hadn't given me that, the fish would—"

"Would what?" asked Ernie.

"Would have died. There was this man who hung them up on—"

Ernie's eyes went all dreamy, then he came back to his senses. "Enough!" he said. "We're living through a time of tests and trials and tribulations. There's work to be done and action to be took! Get these silly creatures out of my sight and get to blooming work! NOW!"

Stan ran to his cupboard and put the fish down. He ran back to the machines and rolled up his sleeves. He was happier than he'd been for weeks. He'd had time off; he'd been to the fair; he'd won the most brilliant of prizes.

"Right. What should I do?"

"Stand there. That's right! Turn that. That's right! Push that. That's right! That's the way to do it. Faster, lad. Faster! Faster! They won't put a stop to it. Oh no, they won't ruin the dreams of Ernest Potts!"

"Who won't, Uncle Ernie?" asked Stan as he pushed and pulled and swivelled and turned.

"Never mind that!" said Ernie. "I'll deal with them. You just concentrate on your work, lad. Faster! Faster! That's right! Fish, fish, fish, fish! Machine, machine, machine, machine! That's the way; that's the way to get it done!"

And they worked together, and sang together.

"Fish in buckets and fish in bins,
Chop off their heads and tails and fins . . ."

Their voices blended with the noise of the machines, and their movements blended with the movement of the machines, and fish poured in at one end and tins poured out at the other, and in the fury of the work, Stan and his uncle forgot all their troubles; and after a time Ernie yelled, "Are ye enjoying it, lad? Are ye having a great time?"

Stan laughed and gave him a thumbs up. "Yes, Uncle Ernie! Yes!" he called.

"Great!" said Ernie. "This is work, son! Proper work. Your dad would've been proud of you. This is what it's all about!"

And they hooted with laughter and they worked and sang and were filled with a strange kind of joy. And they were making such a din, they didn't notice Annie coming in.

SEVEN

Annie had a party tea in her shopping bag: cheese straws, sausage rolls, lemonade, chocolate teacakes and a cake with *Happy Birthday* iced on it, and a bag of candles. She pulled a few pallets together for a table. She used fish tin labels as napkins. She set upside-down buckets as chairs. She laid the birthday tea out and it looked so lovely, the loveliest thing there'd been in this house since the canning began. She smiled in satisfaction, then she went to the central control panel, found the enormous lever with **MASTER SWITCH** written on it, reached up, and pulled it down. The machines came to a sudden stop.

"Sabotage!" yelled Ernie. "Get ready to fight back! They won't—"

"It isn't sabotage," said Annie calmly. "It's teatime."

"Teatime?" said Ernie. "Don't you realize we're living through a time of—"

"Through a time of our nephew's birthday," Annie said. "So take a break and come to tea."

Ernie glared, sputtered, gasped. "But there's—"

Annie went over to him and kissed his cheek. "This is special," she said. "So pipe down for once."

Stan detached himself from his machine. Half in a daze, he walked towards the lovely things laid out on the pallets.

Annie clapped her hands. "This is our nephew, Stan," she said to her husband, "and he is rather more important than our fish."

"I've got fish of my own now, Auntie Annie," said Stan. He showed her his goldfish and told the story of how he got them.

"Oh, they're gorgeous!" said Annie. "They're the most beautiful fish in the whole wide world."

Stan put the bucket by the pallets, and as they ate, they kept looking down at the goldfish and praising them. All except Ernie, of course, who couldn't eat at all. The memory of the investigator's visit rushed and rolled and rocked through his brain.

"Calm down, Ernie," Annie kept saying. "Calm down and eat some cake."

But he couldn't calm down. The cake was like

dust in his mouth. How could he tell his family about Clarence P. Clapp? How could he face up to the catastrophe? He clenched his fists tight. He needed a plot, a plan. The goldfish flickered and flashed below him. He dipped his hand into the bucket and felt their tiny tails and fins against his fingers.

"We need a new line," he declared.

"A what?" said Annie.

"We got to move on from pilchards and cod."

"Move on to what?" said Annie. "And why?"

"Cos we're under attack!" said Ernie.

Annie shook her head. "What on earth are you on about, love?"

Suddenly there was a hammering at the front door, then silence.

"What's that?" said Annie. She got up and headed to the door.

"Don't go!" yelled Ernie. "Don't let them in!"

"Don't let *who* in?" said Annie.

"Them!" said Ernie.

"Who?" said Annie. She opened the door.

There was nobody there, just a white van driving quickly away. Then she saw it, a notice nailed to the door.

DAFT

DEPARTMINT For the ABOLISHUN of FISHY THINGS

FURST, LAST & FINAL WORNIN

It is hearby declaired this 31nd day of JOON That a madman nown as Mr. Silent has been discovered to be up to FISHY STUFF in his dwellin at 69 Fish Key Lane, and therefour that the MADMAN and his Family, if eny, is hearby served with a FURST, LAST & FINAL WORNIN. Orl fishy stuff must stop imediately! Uthawise orl Fishy parafinaylia (i.e. mashines and enjins and cabels and pipes and all the utha stuff I seen) will be forcibly removed. PLUS the sed famly will be evicted -i.e. hoyed owt into the street!

syned
CLARENCE P. Clapp Esq.
(envistigator first grade, seven stars, two pips)

PS This is NOT a joak!
PPS BEWAIR! The envistigator will return WITHOUT ANY WORNIN!

YOU HAS BIN WORND!

GOT a Fishy NAYBOR? call 0191 876 5432
WE will sort them owt!

visit our websight: www. DAFT.gov

EIGHT

When he saw the notice, Ernie jumped onto a gutting machine. He waved his fists in the air. "No surrender!" he yelled. "We'll fight them in the bedrooms and we'll fight them in the kitchen and we'll fight them in the hall. We'll build barricades and booby traps. No surrender! No surrender! God and justice are on our side!"

"No, they're not," said Annie. "There's nothing but daftness on our side. Look what we've done to our lovely home!"

"But look what it's brought us," boomed Ernie. "Look at this thriving business. We've got cash in our pockets and food on our table!"

"Table?" yelled Annie. "We haven't even *got* a table!"

Quietly Stan backed into his cupboard with a piece of birthday cake. He crumbled fragments of the cake and fed it to his fish. Their little mouths opened and closed, just like they were singing "Happy Birthday" to him, and Stan softly sang along.

He held his hand in the water and tickled and stroked the goldfish. They rose to the surface and peered out at him with tiny dark eyes.

"You're my best friends," he whispered.

Outside, Ernie thundered about the sales of sardines, the mark-up on mackerel, the profits on pilchards.

Stan shook his head. "Those fish don't matter," he whispered. "Goldfish are the fish that matter. Goldfish are gorgeous. Goldfish are great."

The thirteen fish wriggled and waved in the water, just like they understood. Stan giggled and smiled at them. He was sure that if they could, they'd smile back.

All went deadly quiet outside.

No machines, no chanting or singing, no arguing.

Annie came to Stan's cupboard door. "Your uncle's thinking," she whispered.

"Thinking about what?" Stan whispered back.

"Just thinking," said Annie.

They listened to the silence together for a moment.

"Maybe thinking'll bring him back to his senses," said Annie.

"Let's hope so," said Stan.

And he sighed and smiled, and Annie stroked his hair and the goldfish swam in a little shoal around his hand.

NINE

Well. How can we watch what happens next? How can we read of such dastardly deeds and sinfulness and tragedy?

What could be so awful? You may well ask.

Oh, innocent reader, just do your job and read. Just listen. Just watch. Or close the book and go away. Turn to happier tales. Leave these soon-to-be doom-laden pages behind. Go quickly.

Otherwise read on.

It's deep into the night. All seems calm in 69 Fish Quay Lane. Stan's in his cupboard, fast asleep. He dreams of ducks and fish in a bucket and of a girl's eye peeping through a peephole in the dust. Annie snoozes too. Her dreams are of how things used to be. She holds the hands of her husband and her nephew and they walk and laugh beside the glittering river. There are great half-built ships standing there. There are men at work. There are fish and chip suppers on the quay. There are no fish-canning machines. Ernie's voice is raised in gentle laughter.

Ernie doesn't sleep. He doesn't laugh. He perches on a filleting machine. He thinks and thinks, and as he thinks a vision comes to him—a glorious, wonderful, and awful vision. He knows that he should reject it, that he should ignore it, that he should fight it off.

And he does try, indeed he does.

He mutters to himself. "No." He clenches his fists. "No!"

All around, his machines are slumbering. There are gentle crackles of electricity, gurgles of water, hisses of steam. Ernie knows that the machines are his, that they are waiting, that they will do his will. He knows that they could make his vision real.

But he continues to fight it.

"No. Aargh! I cannot! No!"

The night thickens and deepens, and the vision comes again and again and again; and Ernie mutters, "No. No. *No!*"

And then it's almost dawn. The stillest hour, the deadest hour. The darkest portion of the night.

"No," he whispers once again, but even as he whispers it he's stepping down from the filleting machine; he's tiptoeing past his sleeping wife; he's tiptoeing towards his sleeping nephew's door. He has a frying pan in his hand. And the machines are sighing, half in horror, half in joy, at what their master is about to do.

"Be brave," he whispers to himself as he creeps slowly towards the cupboard door. "Yes, it's dreadful, but it's for the best. Yes, it's cruel, but it'll make us rich. It'll make us famous. Then nobody'll be able to shut us down. Nobody'll ever be able to take nothing from us ever again. Do it, Ernie. Do it. Do it for the future; do it for the family; do it for poor, poor little Stan . . ."

He opens the door. A shaft of moonlight shines in upon the sleeping boy and falls across the bucket. There they are, the beautiful, tender golden ones. By now, Ernie is deep inside his own vision. There's no resistance left. He grins as he reaches down into the water, as he catches the fish one by one, as he puts them one by one into the pan.

He catches twelve. They lie gasping and writhing and squirming in the pan. The thirteenth dodges and dives in the water, flicking free of Ernie's fingers again and again. He clicks his tongue and grunts.

"Keep still, you pesky—"

The boy stirs in his sleep. Ernie crouches still as a statue, hardly breathes. The twelve fish suck at the air in frantic agony and silence. The boy sleeps on. Ernie slithers backwards, crawls out through the door.

"Come with me, my lovely ones," he whispers. He hurries to his machines. "This won't hurt a bit," he says.

He presses buttons, flicks levers, switches switches. He grins. He clenches his fists. He leaps with joy as the machines come back to vivid life, and begin to do his work.

Ten

It's daylight when Stan wakes. There's no alarm, no hooter, no wakey-wakey. He rubs his eyes. "Am I late?" he says.

Then he looks down into his deserted bucket. The single fish rises from its depths. And as its mouth goes *O* and *O* and *O* and *O*, Stan hears its voice somewhere in his brain.

My companions, weeps the fish.

"Your companions!" answers Stan. "Where are they?"

The fish swims sideways, turns away its face. *They are taken!*

"Taken? What do you mean, taken? Taken by who?"

But there is no answer. The fish swims down to the bottom of the bucket in grief and silence.

There is a cry from outside.

A cry of dreadful joy, of triumph.

"Yes! YES! YES! **YES!**"

"Oh, no!" cries Annie.

"YES!" cries Ernie.

Stan stands up, opens his door.

His uncle turns to him. "Here it is!" he cries. "Our new line!"

And he holds up the little tin with the great golden writing on it: *Potts's Gorgeous Glittering Goldfish.*

Eleven

What would *you* do? Jump for joy that your uncle was so clever? Go for him with your feet and fists? Say "I forgive you, Uncle Ernie. I know that your actions, though sadly misguided, arise from the best of intentions."? Would you beat the earth in anguish? Would you scream in pain? Would you howl with rage? Would you stamp and hiss and snarl and spit?

Stan? He did none of these things. The horror of the tin transfixed him. He couldn't move; he couldn't speak. Ernie cradled the tin in his hands and murmured about a golden future. Stan's eyes glazed over as his uncle talked of shop shelves stacked with gourmet goldfish tinned by Ernest Potts. He talked of diners nibbling Potts's Gorgeous Glittering Goldfish at the Ritz.

Annie went over to her nephew. She tried to hold him to her breast, but he couldn't move. He was a statue. His heart beat to the rhythm of the tragic

words of the thirteenth fish: *My companions! My companions! O my lost companions!*

Then Stan blinked, coughed, reached down, and lifted his bucket.

"I think I'll go for a walk, Auntie Annie," he said.

"A walk?"

"Yes, a walk."

Ernie smiled. "Good idea, lad!" he said. "Stretch your legs. Clear your head. Get a breath of fresh air." He winked at Annie. "See?" he said. "He'll get over it, won't you, lad?"

Ernie stepped aside as Stan brushed past him. He reached out to tousle Stan's hair. Stan turned his face to him.

"I'd rather you didn't do that," he said quietly. He opened the front door.

"Stan?" called Annie. "Stan?"

"I'll be fine," said Stan.

"See?" said Ernie. "Give the lad some time on his own. That's what he needs." Then he had an idea. "Hey, Stan! You could go back to the fair. Get some more of those little beauties for me. Two tons or so should do it! Ha, ha, ha, ha, ha, ha, ha! Tinned goldfish! They'll knock sardines off the shelves!

They'll topple tuna! They'll annihilate the ancho-
vies! Tinned blooming goldfish! I'm a total wonder!
I'm a fishy genius! Fame and fortune's just around
the corner. . . . Ha, ha! Ha, ha, ha, ha, ha, ha!"

Stan turned, took one last look at his uncle and
aunt, and walked away.

TWELve

Annie stood at the door and called Stan's name as he walked off down the road. Should she pursue her dejected nephew? Or should she turn back and try to calm her husband? She teetered on the doorstep. Other eyes watched Stan, those of Clarence P. Clapp, Esq. The DAFT van was half-hidden in an alleyway at the end of the street. Clarence P. pressed a beady eye to his telescope. He pointed it at Stan, then pointed it at the open door of 69 Fish Quay Lane.

"Disgracious," he muttered. "Absolutely appallin'." He leaned back. "It is indeed just as I thunk, lads."

For this time, Clarence P. was not alone. He had the DAFT Squad with him, squeezed into the van, four burly blokes dressed in black with shaved skulls and thick necks and massive hands. Their names were Doug and Alf and Fred and Ted.

"Take a look, lads," said Clarence, and the DAFT Squad jostled to get at the telescope. "What d'you thunk of that, then?" he asked them.

Doug said it was disgustin'.

Alf said it was appallin',

Fred said it was flippin' terrible, boss.

Ted shook his head. He took a deep breath. "Boss," he said, "I sees now that you is right in all you has telled us. The world these days is goin' to Rackanruwin. It will be a honour to teach them people a lesson and hoy them into the street and smash their faces in."

"Well said, Ted," said Clarence P. "His Grand Fishiness of Fishy Things would be proud of you. Now, lads, get warmed up."

And the blokes started to touch their toes and swing their arms and jog on the spot, and the van shook and jerked and squeaked. Distracted by the strange commotion, Stan paused as he passed by. Clarence P. focused the telescope right on his face.

"Quick, lads," he said. "This is one of them. Take a butcher's at the face of evil."

The lads looked. They grunted and groaned in disgust.

Fred retched. "That is the horriblest thing I has ever saw, boss," he said.

"Well said, Fred," said Ted.

"I'll take him easy," said Alf. "Can I kick his teeth out, boss?"

"No, Alf," said Clarence P. "He is just a minnow. We has bigger fish to fry. Let him go."

And Stan looked down at his bucket and walked on.

Clarence P. opened his briefcase. He took out a piece of paper headed:

DAFT EVICSHON NOATIS

He rubbed his hands. "Right, lads," he said. "Heads up, chests out, backs straight. Out we get."

And the lads of the DAFT Squad muscled their way out onto the pavement.

Stan walked on in the morning light. He walked past the Shipwright's Arms and the Salvation Army hostel and the Oxfam shop. The river glistened below him, and far off was the bright blue sea. As he approached the waste ground, he saw that the fair was being dismantled. The great Ferris wheel lay in sections in the back of a large truck. The horses from the merry-go-round were piled up in a trailer. There was no sign of any hot-dog stalls or candyfloss stalls or Gypsy Rose's ancient caravan. Stan walked among it all. Men swung sledgehammers and ropes and tarpaulins. There were yells and curses and the drone of engines. "Watch yer head, young 'un!" came one cry. "Keep clear, you daft little brat!"

Stan ducked and dodged and walked. He didn't know why he was here, what he hoped to do or find. He was aimless, still stunned. The earth shuddered beneath his feet.

"Ye come back, then?" came a voice.

Dostoyevsky, of course, suddenly walking alongside him.

"Couldn't stay away, eh?"

Stan said nothing. Dostoyevsky walked closer. His arm knocked against Stan's shoulder. He pointed down at the bucket. "Where's the rest, then, eh?"

Stan couldn't answer. Tears came to his eyes. A voice inside him said, *Get away from here. Go home.* Another said, *Keep walking. Walk to the ends of the earth, Stan.*

"Ye come te do some work?" asked Dostoyevsky.

"Are you leaving?" said Stan.

"Indeed we are. The stall's took down, the ducks is packed, the caravan's hooked up."

"Where will you go?"

"Here and there and near and far. All the way across the world and mebbe . . ." He paused and smiled. "Have you come to come away with us, young Stan?"

"No," said Stan, but even as he said it he was wondering if he meant yes.

"I got some nice new fish," said Dostoyevsky. "Lovely bright and shiny ones." He leaned close. "Nitasha'd be pleased to see ye. She dun't say much, but I seen it in her eye. My guess is she's quite taken with you, lad."

Stan said

nothing. Straight ahead was a Land Rover with a caravan attached to it. Hook-a-duck ducks were piled up at the caravan window. Nitasha peered out through the window of the Land Rover. Stan had a sudden vision of himself sitting behind her, driving away from machines and tins of fish, moving free across the world.

"Know what I think?" said Dostoyevsky. "I think you're a lad that's bin cooped up far too long. I think you're a lad that's ready for an adventure. Am I right or am I wrong?"

Stan shrugged.

"There's plenty work for you to do," said Dostoyevsky. "All them little fish to care for. And all them ducks to keep clean. It's up to you, but seems to me you're made for travellin' with a hook-a-duck stall."

Stan sighed. Maybe Dostoyevsky was right. He certainly wasn't made for working fish-canning machines in Fish Quay Lane. What kind of life was that? And what kind of life was it to live with a bloke like Ernie, who could do the dreadful thing he'd done last night? He took a deep breath.

"And of course I'll pay you," said Dostoyevsky.

"Jus' like I said I would."

Stan took another deep breath. *Be brave,* he told himself.

"OK," he said. "I'll come along."

"Good lad!" said Dostoyevsky. He opened the Land Rover door. "Look who's come back to us, Nitasha!"

Nitasha turned her eyes to Stan. She peered at him, just like she was peeping through a peephole. There was a fish tank on the back seat, with a shoal of lovely goldfish in it.

Stan got into the Land Rover.

"That's the style," said Dostoyevsky. "Keep an eye on them fish, lad. Don't want them swillin' out, do we?"

He climbed into the driver's seat, turned the engine on, and began to drive slowly across the bumpy waste ground. He picked up speed as he drove uphill away from the river. Stan peered out. He looked along his own street. He saw his aunt and uncle standing outside their house. There was a heap of pipes and cables all around them. A burly bloke dressed in black stood with his arms folded, blocking the front door.

"Put yer own fish in, if ye wants to," Dostoyevsky told Stan, nodding towards the tank.

Stan dipped his hand into his bucket. He lifted out the little fish, then slid it into the tank.

O my companions! he heard inside him.

Nitasha swivelled in her seat, put her tongue out at Stan.

"Welcome to our little family, Stan," said Dostoyevsky, then he put his foot down and accelerated away from the town, from everything that Stan had ever known.

2.

THE FAIRGROUND

THIRteen

It's nearly time for Pancho Pirelli. He'll soon be
entering the tale. Who's Pancho Pirelli? you may
well ask. The feller's a fishy legend, a piscatorial
genius. He's such an amazing bloke that some
people wonder if he's really human. How can he
do what he does? How can he dodge death time
after time after time after time? He must have gills;
he must have scales; he must have fishy fragments
sparking in his brain; he must have fishy particles
pelting through his blood. He's a man of fish and
legend, and when he does appear he'll turn our
Stan's world inside out and upside down. Right
now, of course, at this particular turning of the
page, Pancho doesn't even know that a lad called
Stanley Potts exists. And Stanley's just as ignorant
of Pancho. But their paths are chosen. They're
headed towards each other. Whether they want it
or not, they're going to meet. It's their destiny. It
won't be long.

In the meantime, here's Stan trundling along
in the Land Rover with Dostoyevsky and Nitasha.

The caravan behind them's rattling and swaying. They're following a road beside the sea. There are dunes and beaches and endless water and a few wooden shacks and a couple of villages. The sun's shining in the blue, blue sky and the sea's glinting and a breeze is blowing and there are boats dancing on the swell and Dostoyevsky's happy as can be.

"This is the life, Stan!" he calls. "The open road! The world's our oyster! We're wild and footloose and we're fancy-free!"

He swerves to avoid a pothole in the road. He beams at Stan in the rear-view mirror.

"What d'ye think, our Stan? How's it feel to be fancy-free?"

Stan looks away. He dips his fingers in the tank. He watches the dunes streaming past. He's already starting to wonder if he's done the wrong thing. Why did he turn his back on everything he loved? What on earth got into him?

Nitasha swivels in her seat and grins. "He's blubbin'!" she says.

"No, I'm not!" says Stan.

Dostoyevsky regards the boy again. "It's natural

to be blubbin'," he says. "Ye'd be blubbin' yerself, Nitasha, if ye'd done what he's jus' done. Is that it, our Stan? Are ye havin' second thoughts, are ye, Stan?"

Stan tries to control his voice. He tries to avoid Nitasha's eyes. "No," he says, but his voice is hardly more than a whisper.

"Are ye missin' yer folks?" continues Dostoyevsky.

Stan meets the man's eye. "Just a little bit, Mr. Dostoyevsky," he says at last.

Nitasha stifles a giggle.

Dostoyevsky winks at Stan in the rear-view mirror. "I know ye must be. But never mind," he says. "Ye'll soon get used to bein' with us. Ye'll soon get used to bein' wild an' free. Ain't that right, Nitasha?"

"Yes!" snorts Nitasha.

Stan looks down. *Be brave,* he tells himself.

"And ye'll soon forget about the folks you left behind," says Dostoyevsky. "Ain't that right, Nitasha?"

"Yes!" snaps Nitasha. "Yes, he will!"

"That's right," says Dostoyevsky. "So stop your

worryin', son. We're yer family now, and we'll look after you."

He puts his foot down. The engine roars. The Land Rover and the hook-a-duck caravan thunder on.

Stan leans back in his seat. He tells himself that he has done the right thing. He tells himself that all will be well. He tells himself he must be brave. But he has to keep on squeezing back the tears.

FouRTeen

They drive and drive. Dostoyevsky and Nitasha
eat pork pies and pick 'n' mix that they get from
a garage on the way. Nitasha lobs sweets over
her shoulder: chocolate peanuts, midget gems,
American hard gums, mints, mini cola bottles,
jelly snakes. They lie on Stan's lap and all around
him on the seat and on the floor. He stares out into
the world that seems wider and wider
the further they go.

"You got te eat," says Dostoyevsky.
"Ye got te keep yer strength up, Stan. It ain't an
easy life, keepin' a hook-a-duck stall on the go."

 So Stan licks Love Hearts that have KISS
ME QUICK and YOU'RE A SWEETIE stamped on
them. He slowly chews a blue
jelly baby. He dangles his
fingers in the fish tank and feels
fins and tails and tiny mouths moving
tenderly against his skin. There's other fairground
traffic on the road. A massive Wall of Death truck
lumbers past them. A camper van chugs along

with a bearded lady and a tattooed lady waving gleefully from the windows. Dostoyevsky waves back and toots his horn.

The day wears on and the light starts to fade. The sun descends towards the darkening sea. There's a town in the distance: spires and sky-scrapers and turrets. Dostoyevsky cheers.

"That's the place!" he yells. "That's the place that's in need of hook-a-duck!"

They enter the outskirts of the town and stop at a red traffic light. A policeman walks into the road and stands in front of them with his hands on his hips.

"Best behaviour, Stan!" hisses Dostoyevsky.

The policeman strolls to the driver's door. "You're with the fair," he says.

"Correct, officer," says Dostoyevsky.

"Name?"

"Wilfred Dostoyevsky, officer. And these is the kids, Stanley and Nitasha."

The policeman comes round to Stan's door. He peers through the window. He opens the door and shines a torch into Stan's face. Stan wants to yell, *Yes! You've caught me! Take me in! Arrest me! I'm*

Stanley Potts, the runaway boy from Fish Quay Lane!
The policeman narrows his eyes. "So you're
Stanley, are you?" he whispers.

"Yes, officer."

"And tell me, Stanley," he says even more softly.
"Are you a troublemaking kind of boy?"

"Course he's not, officer," says Dostoyevsky.
"He's—"

The policeman turns. "Did I ask *you*, Mr.
Dostoyevsky?"

"No, officer," admits Dostoyevsky.

"So keep *out* of it!" He bares his teeth in a kind of
smile. "Are you," he says again, "a troublemaker,
young Stanley?"

"No, sir," whispers Stan.

"Good! Cos do you know what we do with
troublemakers in this town?"

"No, sir," whispers Stan.

"That's good! It's *best* you don't know! Cos you
know what would happen if you *did* know?"

"No, officer," says Stan.

"It would," said the policeman, "scare. . . you. . .
stiff!" He keeps the torch shining onto Stan's face.
"Do you know what I know?" he says.

"No, sir."

"I know lads like you, and I know what lads like you get up to, 'specially in these dark days. In fact, I know all you ragamuffin fairground folk traipsing and wandering across the world and leaving all kinds of bother in your wake. I also know that if I had *my* way. . ." He lowers the torch. "But that's another tale."

The traffic is building up. A car horn sounds. The policeman leans back. He shines the torch towards the car that's just behind.

"Sorry, officer!" comes a frightened call. "My mistake! Didn't see you there!"

The policeman scribbles something in a notebook. He points towards a side road with his torch. He glares at Dostoyevsky.

"That's where we're sending you lot," he says. "Down to the waste ground. Down to where the dumps are. That's where your silly fair'll be happening. That's where you'll stay. There and nowhere else. And once it's *over*. . ."

"Once it's over," says Dostoyevsky, "we'll clear up and we'll be on our way."

"Correct. And if there's any *trouble*. . ."

"And if there's any trouble, then we'll pay."

"I see you've been in this line of work a long time, Mr. Dostoyevsky."

"Man and boy," says Dostoyevsky.

The policeman sneers and shakes his head. "What a stupid waste of life. Go on. Get going. And I don't want to see you and your troublemaking kids again. Go!"

Dostoyevsky drives on, into the dark potholed side road.

"It's always the same, Stan," he says. "They treat us like an affliction, when they should welcome us as a blessin'. Tek no notice."

There are overhanging trees and high hedges on either side. The road becomes a slippery dirt track, then it opens up into a space where fires burn and smoke curls up into the sky. There are Land Rovers and caravans and dogs scampering and kids running and music playing.

"Here we are," says Dostoyevsky. "We'll take care of ye, Stan. Me and my Nitasha. Won't we, love?"

FIFTEEN

Now here's the thing about Stanley Potts. He hasn't exactly had it easy, has he? Life hasn't been a bed of roses. He's hardly traipsing down a primrose path. It ain't quite been a piece of cake. No way. But the thing about Stan is, he's got the single most important thing: a good heart. And if you've got a good heart—like *most* kids have when it comes down to it—then you'll survive.

So here's Stan with his strange new family in a bumpy field, in a far-off town, and he's surrounded by a bunch of what some folk would call vagabonds and weirdos. Dostoyevsky parks the caravan. They wander through the field. As they walk, there are voices calling out of the darkness and out of caravan windows.

"It's Dostoyevsky and Nitasha! How ye doing, Wilfred? How's things, Nitasha? How's the hook-a-duck trade?"

And Dostoyevsky's waving and calling back his greetings, and a couple of times he puts his arm round Stan's shoulders and cries out, "This is me new lad, Stan! He's a good fine lad!"

And the voices call back, "Hello there, Stan! Welcome to the fair, son!"

They pass fiddle players and a snake charmer and a trio of boys standing on one another's shoulders. They sit down by a glowing fire. There's a ring of people around it, their faces shining in its light. A man leans down and reaches into the embers with a pair of tongs. He holds something out to Stan, something black and round and smoking.

"Tek it," he says in a gruff voice. "It's fer ye. Go on, lad."

Stan stares at it, doesn't move.

The bloke laughs. "Go *on*," he says again.

"Go *on*," says Dostoyevsky.

Nervously Stan reaches out and takes the thing. It's hard and black and scorching hot. He gasps, drops it, picks it up again. The people around the fire laugh.

"Chuck it up and down," instructs Dostoyevsky. "It'll cool it."

So Stan throws it up and down and rolls it around his palm.

"Now crack it open," says the bloke.

Stan presses with his thumb. It's still mad hot and he can still hardly hold it. But he presses again and the thing cracks open. Some of the black crust falls away and Stan sees there's a beautiful white inside, and now there's steam mixed with the smoke and it smells delicious.

"A *potato!*" he whispers.

"Correct," says the bloke. "It's a spud."

Stan lifts it to his mouth and nibbles, and he tastes the soft creamy smokiness of it. He looks at the faces around the fire and they all look back at him and grin. He eats again. It's the loveliest thing he's ever tasted. Dostoyevsky laughs and puts his arm round him. Stan sighs and eats and starts to relax. He finds he's smiling. He looks at Nitasha and she seems happier and a little bit prettier.

They continue to sit there. They eat more spuds. Somebody puts a tin mug of tea in Stan's hands.

"So where ye from, young Stan?" asks a bloke across the fire.

"Fish Quay Lane," says Stan.

"The town we was in yesterday," Dostoyevsky

explains. "They've had it tough back there. Ship-yards shut, blokes on the dole, all that stuff."

"Needed a new life, did ye?" says the bloke.

"That's right," says Dostoyevsky.

"Well, ye've come te the right place, Stan," says a woman whose necklaces and bangles glitter in the firelight. "Ye're with pals here."

Another woman in another part of the field sings a lovely foreign song. Dostoyevsky and the others at the fire talk. They talk of fairs they remember and of fairs they know through legend and myth. Somebody brings a crate of beer to the fireside, and as they drink they talk of magic acts and escapologists and two-headed goats and of those who can talk to the dead. They talk in strange accents from far-flung places and faraway lands. Stan listens and loses himself in the voices that flash and flicker like the flames. He loses himself in the tales that move like weird shadows through the air. After a time a great full moon lifts over the field and bathes everything in its strange silver light.

"They say Pancho Pirelli's on his way," says one of the voices.

"Pirelli? Thought he was in Madagascar or Zanzibar or somewhere."

"I thought he was dead."

"Seems he was spotted on the road, somewhere in the north."

"Pancho? Comin' here? Can't be nothin' but a rumour."

"He's never been nothin' but a rumour. All that stuff that's said about him. Pah!"

"Ye'll believe it when ye see it."

"There's nothin' te believe. He's a showman, a trickster."

"Ye're wrong. He's one of the greats."

"Was," says someone else. *"Was* one of the greats. *Was* extraordinary. But even Pancho Pirelli has te get old, has te lose his old magic, has te . . ."

The voice doesn't finish the sentence. They all sigh Pancho's name and shake their heads in wonder.

"Who *is* Pancho Pirelli?" Stan dares to ask.

"You'll see," says Dostoyevsky. "If he turns up, you'll see, and you'll not have seen nothin' like it never before."

They all nod at that, and move on to talk of other things.

SIXTeen

They stay by the fire. Deep into the night, Stan whispers to Dostoyevsky, "Mr. Dostoyevsky, I think I need the toilet."

"You *think* you need the toilet?" he replies.

"I mean I *do* need the toilet."

"The boy needs the *toilet!*" Dostoyevsky calls.

"The lavatory!" comes another voice.

"The khazi, the thunderbox, the loo, the netty, the bog!"

Stan feels his face burning. "Where is it?" he whispers.

"It's out there in the dark," says Dostoyevsky. "If it's a number two, go downwind and dig a ditch." He touches Stan's arm gently. "It's OK. There'll be a proper place tomorrow. Go to the edge of the field. We'll keep an eye out for ye comin' back."

Laughter follows Stan as he stands up and leaves. He shuffles away from the fire. He stumbles over car tracks and holes and tussocks of grass. He smells potatoes and beer and pies and horse dung and woodsmoke and pipe smoke. A little

dog sniffs at his heels. A couple of scrawny half-
naked kids call out to him, "Who are ye? What's
yer name?"

"Stan," says Stan.

"And what ye doin' here?"

"I'm with the hook-a-duck stall," answers Stan,
and he surprises himself by feeling a little flicker
of pride.

"Aha!" say the kids, impressed.

Stan goes beyond the fires to the deeper dark at
the edge of the field.

"I said we'd meet again," comes a gentle voice.

Stan turns. A woman's standing there, wearing a
long dress and a headscarf. Her face shines in the
light of the moon.

"Gypsy Rose," she says. "Remember?"

"Yes," says Stan.

"I said that you would travel. Remember?"

"Yes," says Stan.

"And you must have done so, for here you are,
so far away. I remember that your name is Stan."
She moves closer. She holds his chin, gently turns
his face towards the moon. "Let me look into your
eyes. Ah, yes, I see that you are still entranced.

And I see that you have become dejected, as I said you would."

Stan can't move. He doesn't know whether to run, to call out, or just to stay where he is.

"Don't worry, Stan," murmurs Gypsy Rose. "I am no danger to you. Do you have silver with which to cross my palm?"

"I've got nothing," he says.

"Nothing? That's not quite true, is it, Stan? You have yourself. You have your good heart. Always remember that. Now, let us say that the moonlight is your silver." She opens her hand and lets the moonlight fall across her palm. "Thank you for it, Stan. Now, open your own hand and let me look into it."

She takes his hand and opens it and lets the moonlight fall on it. He looks down at the lines and tiny creases and cracks and bulges there.

"Moonlight is the best of all," says Gypsy Rose. "It gives the purest, most truth-telling light."

She traces the lines on his palm with her fingertip. "Oh, Stanley," she murmurs. "There have already been disastrous moments in your short life. But you will live long. And better times will

come if you can overcome
the perils that lie in wait."

"Perils?" whispers Stan.

"What is the purpose of living
if there are no perils to be encountered
and overcome?" She smiles. Stan can't answer
her. "I see water," she continues. "I see great
peril there." She leans closer. "But you must
be brave. You must say yes. Much gold could
be yours. Do not be troubled by the teeth."

"Troubled by the . . ."

"I don't know what that means. But I do know
that you left someone behind, Stan."

"Yes. My aunt and uncle. Annie and Ernie. Can
you see what is happening to them?"

Gypsy Rose shakes her head. "No. But perhaps
your heart and the moon will draw them to you."

"The moon?"

"The moon is filled with the yearning of human
hearts, Stan. Have you noticed how it burns brightest when we ache with longing?"

Stan has no answer. Is it true? He gazes now up
into the moon and thinks of his absent aunt and
uncle; and yes, its light does seem to intensify.

"Annie and Ernie look upon the same moon as you, Stan," says Gypsy Rose. "Do they have good hearts too?"

"Yes," says Stan. Then he thinks of Ernie and the tin of goldfish and he turns his eyes towards the earth. "But . . ."

"But they have made mistakes."

"Yes."

"As we all do. If their hearts are good and true, the light of the moon that is filled with your yearning will draw them to you. Now, you were on an errand, I believe."

Stan gulps. "I need to pee," he whispers.

"Then go," says Gypsy Rose. "Look. There are some shadows beneath those old trees there."

Stan turns from her. He slips into the shadows under the trees and pees into the silvery dark. When he returns, she's gone. And the dark shape of Dostoyevsky is moving through the field, calling his name.

SEVENTEEN

That night, when they return to the caravan at last, Stan lies on a bench beneath a blanket with the thirteenth fish and its companions at his side. The moon shines through the little caravan window and he gazes up and sends his yearning through the night. Then he sleeps, and in his dreams angry policemen shine torches into his eyes and warn him that he'd better be good. A glowing fire rises from the earth and turns into the moon. Voices drone and whisper and laugh and sing. He sees giants and dwarfs and three-headed sheep. A strongman lifts him up, throws him into the sky, and catches him as he falls. A man with a tiger on his back chases him into a forest. Ducks spin in circles round his head. He finds himself deep in water, swimming, and there's a fin on his back. *My companions!* he cries. *O where are my companions?* He sees Annie and Ernie walking along the road beside the sea. They look ancient and wizened and worn. He calls to them. He reaches out to them, and then comes a voice from far, far away:

"COME ON! UP! SIX O'CLOCK AND TIME TO START!"

Stan leaps from his sleep. Is he back in Fish Quay Lane? Is the fish-canning about to begin? No, he's in the caravan. The voice is Dostoyevsky's.

"It's six o'clock, Stan. There's a hook-a-duck stall to put up. It's time to start."

Eighteen

It's easy to assemble a hook-a-duck stall, especially one that's been assembled so many times in so many places for so many years. Stan sets to work with Dostoyevsky. Bolt the wooden boards together, hoist a few poles for the canopy, sling the canopy over the top, tie down the canopy with a few ropes. Stand back. Admire. Read the scarlet lettering:

The FAMOUS DOSTOYEVSKY's HOOK - A - DUCK
∧ PRIZE EV'RY TIME!

Then get the plastic pool for the plastic ducks and place it at the centre.

Stan enjoys it once he gets going, just like he always enjoys himself when he's hard at work. He runs back and forth to a tap at the edge of the field. He collects water in a bucket and fills up the pool. As he runs he finds he already has friends — people who call out his name and wave.

All around, stalls and sideshows are being set up. The sun shines down. The fair grows by the hour. There are merry-go-rounds with teacups for the little ones. There are dodgems and a carousel. There's a haunted house, a ghost train, Dracula's castle. There are shooting galleries and coconut shies. There are hot dogs and chips and burgers and sides of beef and legs of pork. Stan sees Gypsy Rose's caravan with the little pony tethered near it, and more caravans with Gypsy names painted on the sides. He fills up the pool; he cleans the ducks; he sets them on the water. He gets the rods and the hooks and lays them out ready for customers. He takes goldfish from the tank and puts them in plastic bags with plenty of water. As he hangs them up above the stall, he whispers that he'll make sure they go to good homes. He doesn't lift out the thirteenth fish, of course. It swims elegantly through the tank, whispering farewell to its companions.

Dostoyevsky applauds when it's all done. He sees Nitasha peeping out from the caravan window and points at Stan like he's really proud of him. Nitasha scowls.

"Ye're a natural, Stan," he says. "It's like ye was born fer it."

Stan finds some paper and a pen. He sits on the grass and carefully makes some certificates. He uses his best handwriting:

I hereby promise that I will take good care of this lovely littel fish. I will give it fresh water and food and love.
Signed _ _ _ _ _ _ _ _ _ _ _ _ _ _ _ _ _
Date _ _ _ _ _ _ _ _ _ _ _ _ _ _ _ _ _

Nitasha comes out of the caravan. She's bleary-eyed and wearing a dirty old nightie.

"What's this?" she says. She picks up one of the certificates. She reads it and snorts. "Love!" she says. "*Love!* Huh! D'ye think they'll take any notice of this once they're out of yer sight?"

"Yes," says Stan. "They have to promise."

She snorts again. "Promise!"

"Tek no notice, Stan," says Dostoyevsky. He contemplates his daughter, and shakes his head. "She used te be a lovely lass."

"Used to be? *Used* to be!" echoes Nitasha.

"But that," says Dostoyevsky, "was in the time of *Mrs.* Dostoyevsky."

Nitasha glares. She stamps back to the caravan, goes inside, slams the door.

"*Mrs.* Dostoyevsky?" says Stan.

"Aye," says Dostoyevsky. "Me wife. Nitasha's mother. She went off to Siberia with a troupe of ballerinas. She never came back."

The caravan door swings open. Nitasha leans out. "She said she'd take me with her, if you must know!" she snaps. She glares at Stan. "What do you think of *that*?"

"I don't know," says Stan.

"Then she said I hadn't practised enough! So what did she do?"

"She went off to Siberia?" asks Stan.

"Yes! She went off to *Siberia*!" Nitasha slams the door again.

"Siberia?" asks Stan.

"More than a year ago," says Dostoyevsky.

The door swings open. "I hope she's stuck in a snowdrift!" yells Nitasha. "I hope she's turned to ice!" The door slams shut.

"To be honest, Stan," admits Dostoyevsky, "I think Mrs. Dostoyevsky was a bit disappointed in me. She had dreams and ambitions and I don't really think the hook-a-duck was good enough for her. Anyway, Nitasha's not been the same since."

The door swings open again. Nitasha stamps towards Stan. "This is a picture of her, if ye *must* see!"

Stan takes the photograph. It shows a slender woman with flowing hair in a flowing dress leaping through the air.

"She looks lovely," he says.

"Lovely!" snorts Nitasha. She snatches the photograph from him.
"Here," she says. "Give it back before ye ruin it." She stamps back to the caravan and slams the door.

Dostoyevsky shrugs. The door swings open once more.

"She *was* lovely!" yells Nitasha.

Then the door slams shut again.

Stan feels a tug at his arm. A little boy's standing there. "Can I try to hook a duck, please, mister?" he asks.

"She *was!*" yells Nitasha from behind the closed door.

NINETEEN

Stan loves that first hook-a-duck morning. It's all
so different from the crazy crowded house in Fish
Quay Lane. Little groups and families make their
way across the field, between the rides and stalls.
Music belts out from the waltzer. There's screaming from the roller coaster that thunders across the
sky. The little boy's the first of many that come to
the stall. Stan wears a money belt around his waist.
Soon there are lots of notes zipped into it, and it's
heavy with coins. Stan helps the kids with the rods
and hooks. Once or twice he has to guide their
hand as they sign the certificates. He looks into
their eyes; he asks them to promise that they really
will take care of the fish. Only one person objects,
the dad of a little girl dressed in red and green.
The girl lifts a duck from the pool; she squeaks
with delight; Stan lifts down a little fish and asks
her to sign, please.

"Sign *what*?" says the bloke.

"A certificate," says Stan.

The man and his daughter read it. The girl

reaches for a pencil but the man twists his face.

"Don't do it," he says.

"But she's got to," says Stan.

"Says who?" says the bloke.

"Me," says Stan.

"And *why*?"

"Because . . . because . . ."

Stan starts trembling. The bloke's got a thick neck with a silver chain around it. LOVE and HATE are tattooed on his knuckles. He's got big glaring eyes that stare at Stan. He's got big, strong fingers that poke Stan in the chest. He's got a deep, surly voice that snarls, "We don't sign nowt unless we got to."

"But . . ." says Stan.

"Are you suggestin'," snarls the bloke, "that me and my Minnie might be cruel?"

"No," says Stan. "But . . ."

"Good," says Minnie's dad. "So give her the fish."

Dostoyevsky's leaning against the caravan, watching. He doesn't move. Stan looks at him, then back at the bloke. He holds the plastic bag with the fish in it. The bloke looms over him. Stan's hardly as high as the man's chest.

"Give. Her. The. *Fish*."

Stan takes a deep breath. He holds the bag up. The fish swims its lovely little circles and figures of eight. "It's just . . ."

"It's just," says the bloke, "a stupid *fish*. What's so special about a stupid *fish*?"

"It's so little . . ." says Stan.

"Ah, poor ickle fish."

"It's so little and we are so big," says Stan. "It's so easy to hurt it. It's . . ."

The bloke sighs. He curses. Stan holds the fish higher. Sunlight pours into the little plastic bag and the fish glitters and glows.

Minnie steps closer.

"Just look how lovely it is," Stan tells her.

Minnie stares, like she's seeing a fish for the first time.

"Look at the scales," says Stan. "Look at the feathery fins and tail. Look how it curves and curls through the water. Look at its shining eyes."

"It's beautiful," says Minnie in wonder. "Look, Dad, it's like it's saying O O O O. And it's so little, and so delicate, and so . . ."

And even the man, listening to his daughter and

staring into the plastic bag, seems to be entranced, if only for a split second.

"It's lovely," says Minnie. "Let's just sign, Dad, and take it home."

The man curses under his breath. He sighs. "OK," he grunts at last. "OK, just get it signed and let's move on."

Minnie signs the certificate. *Minnie*. She smiles at Stan. Stan smiles back.

"Thank you very much," he says. "Do come back and try your luck again."

Minnie walks away happily with her dad, whispering to her fish.

"Well done," says Dostoyevsky, coming over. "Yer very first awkward customer and ye dealt with it very well. Ye'll come across a million more." He rubs his hands. He reaches into Stan's money belt and starts to count the notes and coins. "Ye're doin' great. Ye're a natural, like I said."

More customers come. Soon there's only one fish left hanging on the stall in its plastic bag, and only a couple left swimming in the tank with the thirteenth fish. Stan's sad that so

many are gone, but he's pleased as well. He's been hatching what he thinks is the perfect plan.

"Mr. Dostoyevsky," he says.

"Aye, lad?"

"I was thinking. Now that all the fish are nearly gone . . ."

"Aye, lad?"

"Well, I thought that maybe we could offer different kinds of prizes."

"*Dif'rent* prizes?"

"Yes. Like cuddly toys or bags of sweets or—"

"Cuddly *toys* or bags of *sweets*?" says Dostoyevsky. He looks at Stan in astonishment and shakes his head. "Ye really have got a lot to learn. It's *tradition*, lad. Ye hook a plastic duck at Dostoyevsky's and ye get a fish. It's how it is and how it's been and how it will always be!"

"But, Mr. Dostoyevsky, there's hardly any fish left."

"So we get some more!"

Stan holds up his hands. "But where *from*, Mr. Dostoyevsky?"

"From the *goldfish supplier*!"

Stan looks blank. "*What* goldfish supplier?" he asks.

"Dear, dear, *dear*! From the goldfish supplier at the *fair*!"

Stan just stares at him.

"Listen, Stan. Every fair has a goldfish supplier. Where else d'ye think all the goldfish come from? *Thin air?*"

"I don't know," admits Stan.

"Exactly. Ye've got a lot to learn. But I s'pose that's how it has to be." Dostoyevsky takes Stan's money belt from him and gives Stan a handful of coins. "Find the supplier and buy some more fish."

Stan looks across the crowded field. "Where *is* the supplier?" he says.

"Ain't got a clue. Somewhere. Findin' him'll be part of yer trainin'."

"And how many should I get?" asks Stan.

"Half a shoal."

"Half a shoal? But how many's in a shoal?"

"How should I know? Seems to depend on how the fish is feelin' on the day. There's tiny shoals and medium-size shoals and shoals as big as the sea. Tell him you're buyin' for Dostoyevsky and the supplier'll help ye out."

"How much do I pay?"

Dostoyevsky shrugs. "Same thing. Tell him they're for Dostoyevsky and ye'll get a proper price." He puts his hands on his hips. "That's enough questions, lad. Go on. Off ye go."

"You won't give the thirteenth fish away?" says Stan.

"No, Stan."

"You promise?"

"You want me to sign a certificate?"

Stan shakes his head.

"Go on, then," says Dostoyevsky.

"OK," says Stan. He turns away.

"Cuddly *toys*!" mutters Dostoyevsky. "Bags of bloomin' *sweets*!"

TWENTY

As Stan walks through the fair, he has the weirdest feeling that he's being watched. He looks around, but there are just the usual kids and dogs and families and stallholders. Every now and then somebody waves or calls his name. He waves back. He keeps on walking. He keeps on having the feeling, like there's one pair of eyes that's picked him out from all the people at the fair, one pair of eyes that's following him. It's not a scary feeling. It's just a bit . . . weird.

He looks for signs of the goldfish supplier. A woman outside the haunted house pulls a pair of fangs from her mouth and says he seems a bit lost. He tells her what he's looking for.

"Fish?" she says. "Can't help you there, lad. There's no call for fish in the fiend and phantom trade. Unless they're dead, of course." She puts the fangs back in and raises her clawed hands and howls like a wolf and pretends to chase him off.

Stan carries on.

"I'm Tickle Peter," says a man who comes to walk at his side.

"I'm Stan," says Stan. "Do you know where the goldfish supplier is?"

"Make me laugh and I might tell you."

Stan stops and looks at him. Peter's wearing leopard-skin trunks and a pair of silver braces. On his head is a pointed hat with *Tickle Peter and Make Him Laugh and Win £100* written on it. He holds out a bag.

"Only costs a pound. Use one of these feathers or a stick or a leaf or whatever you want. Tickle me, make me laugh, and you'll win a hundred pounds. Then I'll tell you what I know about the feller you're looking for."

Tickle Peter goes silent. His face is glum. He waits for Stan to respond. Stan thinks about the pound. Is it right to spend a pound to try to get the information?

"Or you can tell me a joke, if you know any," says Peter. He sighs. "I haven't laughed for twenty years. Go on, Stan. Make me laugh."

Stan puts his hand into his pocket, takes out a pound coin and gives it to Peter. "Why did the monkey fall out of the tree?" he says. It's the only joke he knows. He remembers it from those far-off days at school. He remembers laughing and laughing when he heard it.

"I don't know," says Tickle Peter. His face turns even glummer. He sighs. "Why *did* the monkey fall out of the tree?"

"Because it was dead!" cries Stan.

Peter sighs again. "Is that it?" he says.

"Yes," says Stan. "Have you heard it before?"

"Once or twice. Listen. I'm feeling generous. You can tell me another one."

Stan looks down.

"You don't know any more, do you?" says Peter.

Stan shakes his head.

"Try a tickle, then." Peter holds out the bag again.

Stan chooses a long, brightly coloured feather. Peter raises his arms and Stan tickles his armpits. He tickles him behind the knees. He tickles him on the chest and on the legs and on the neck.

Peter doesn't move. His face turns ever glummer.

"Enough," he says at last. "I thought you might have it in you, Stan, but clearly you haven't. What a disappointment."

Stan puts the feather back in the bag.

"It's my living," explains Peter. "I've made a fortune from all the pounds I've taken over the years. But I'd give it all away if only I could laugh." He shrugs and turns to go. "Maybe I'll see you around, Stan."

"You could still tell me about the goldfish supplier," says Stan.

Peter pauses. "I could."

"Go on, then. Please?"

"OK, I don't know anything about any goldfish supplier."

"But you said—"

"I said I'd tell you what I know about the bloke you're looking for. And what I know is nothing." Tickle Peter watches Stan. "See what happens when you don't laugh for twenty years? See what happens when you make your living by tricking and cheating? You turn cruel and bitter, Stan, that's what happens. Good-bye."

Stan kicks the grass. He spits. He spins around, and there, right behind him, where before there was just an empty space, is a sign stuck to a post that's been stabbed into the earth.

DIRECTIONS TO THE
GOLDFISH SUPPLIER

Past the clattering dodgems,
beyond the penny Falls,
First right at the Ferris wheel,
then past the groaning wrestling
booth, where you must call out
in a loud voice,
"PIN HIM DOWN, THUNDERER!"
Then eat a piece of boar
at the Wild Boar Cookhouse
and head for the tent which
looks like the WORLD.
Whistle "It's a Long Way to
Tipperary" and there you will be.

TWENTY-ONE

Stan follows the directions. They take him through the heart of the fair. The wrestling booth has a great arched entrance decorated with paintings of ancient wrestlers. The painted wrestlers wear masks and capes and some pose with their arms folded and others with their arms raised to show off their muscles. They grapple with each other. They fly feet first through the air. There is a great roar from the hidden crowd inside the booth. There are loud gasps of horror and astonishment. There's a sudden silence in the roar, into which Stan calls, "Pin him down, Thunderer!" Then comes a great round of cheering and applause, and a victory has obviously been won. Stan walks on and finds himself at the Wild Boar Cookhouse.

A whiskery man who looks like a boar himself leans down from the counter and holds out a piece of meat. "Have a chop, sonny," he grunts.

Stan takes it from the man's hairy hand. He chews the delicious meat and licks the delicious juices from his lips.

"Is it luvly enuff?" growls the boar man.

"It is," says Stan.

"What ye after?" says the boar man.

"A tent," answers Stan.

The boar man grunts. "Have ye heard the tale about the man that et the boar?"

Stan shakes his head.

"He ended up as a boar hisself. Have ye heard the tale about the boar that et the man?"

"It ended up as a man itself?"

"Mebbe it would of. Mebbe it *should* of. That would make sense. But no, it was hunted down and shot."

"That's a pity," says Stan, thinking about the family of the boar.

"Is it?" says the boar man. "It turned out very tasty." He points to the meat in Stan's hand. "As you can testify yourself. Now here's another. Have ye heard the tale of the tent that looked like the world?"

Stan shakes his head.

"It ended up lookin' nowt like a tent."

Stan swallows the last of the meat. He licks his fingers. "What does that mean?" he says.

"It means ye should be whistlin' by now."

Stan starts whistling "It's a Long Way to Tipperary," and a man appears from among the trees and beckons Stan towards him.

"Are you the goldfish supplier?" asks Stan.

"Do I *look* like the goldfish supplier?" asks the man.

"I don't know," says Stan.

"Then what *do* I look like?"

"I don't know. Like a man."

"Like a man? That's good. You can stop whistling that horrible tune now. Come along."

And the man reaches towards a tree, and draws it towards him, and Stan realizes that what looks like trees is in fact the canvas walls of a tent with images of trees and earth and sky on them.

"I thought it was trees!" Stan gasps.

Behind him, the boar man snuffles and grunts.

"Of course you did," says the man at his side. "You thought it was trees. You thought it was the world. But it is not. It is just a tent. Now hurry up and get inside. My name is Mr. Smith, by the way."

"I'm Stan," says Stan.

"Come *along*," says Mr. Smith.

TWENTY-TWO

The inside of the tent is cavernous. There are true trees growing there and Stan touches them and, yes, they're real. The light is dim, like dawn. Mr. Smith walks briskly, hurrying Stan forward. They pass huge empty cages whose steel bars are all rusted.

"Elephants," says Mr. Smith when he sees Stan looking.

"Elephants?" says Stan.

"There used to be elephants in the cages. And lions and tigers and zebras and bears. But that was in the old days when we supplied everything. It's all come to an end except for goldfish and a few speciality items. Hurry along, please. And be careful where you step. There are rumours that a pair of scorpions have escaped."

Stan stares down in horror at the ground beneath his feet. "Scorpions?" he gasps. "Why do you have *scorpions*?"

"For the scorpion act, of course. And if you hear flapping, be sure to duck. It'll be the eagle. He likes to land on heads, and his claws are very long and very, *very* sharp."

Stan looks at the earth. He looks at the sky. He holds his hands against his skull, and his heart thunders and thumps.

"Goodness gracious," says Mr. Smith. "I can see that you are not used to this. What on earth are you doing here?"

Stan gasps again. He goggles at the man. What is he doing here? How on earth did he end up like this? He wants to yell:

"I'M JUST AN ORDINARY BOY!
I DON'T WANT TO BE IN A TENT THAT
**LOOKS LIKE THE WORLD, SEARCHING
FOR HALF A SHOAL OF GOLDFISH!**
**I DON'T WANT TO BE FRIGHTENED OF
SCORPIONS AND EAGLES! I WANT
TO GO RIGHT BACK TO THE
START, WHEN I HAD AN
ORDINARY LIFE WITH AN
ORDINARY FAMILY IN
AN ORDINARY HOME
AND I WAS ORDINARY
LITTLE STANLEY
POTTS!"**

The yelling inside his head feels so loud that Stan is certain Mr. Smith must hear it.

"Well?" says Mr. Smith.

Stan sighs. "Wilfred Dostoyevsky sent me here," he whispers.

Mr. Smith nods. "That makes sense," he says. "Now come along. Aargh! Look out! Duck!"

Stan flings himself to the ground and wraps his arms around his head. Nothing happens. He hears laughter. He looks up.

"My little joke," says Mr. Smith. "Works every time. Now get up. The goldfish supplier's ready for you."

And he walks away.

TWENTY-THREE

The goldfish supplier is sitting at a desk in front of an assortment of plastic ponds. A fishing net is slung over his shoulder. He grins and beckons Stan towards him.

"You found me. Well done. That's half the battle over. I'm Seabrook. What's your name and what's your poison?"

"Poison?" says Stan.

"Forgive me. You're new, aren't you? Seabrook's way is we have a drink and a chinwag, then we get down to business. I can do you water, fizzy water, or black pop."

Stan suddenly realizes that he's very thirsty. "What's in the black pop?" he asks.

Seabrook taps his nose and winks. "Something  black," he says. "Something secret. Something delicious." He reaches into a drawer in the desk and takes out a squat glass bottle filled with black stuff and hands it to Stan.

"Some folk say it makes them do

sums better," says Seabrook. "Some folk say it makes them run better." He twists his nose. "Some folk even say it helps them to drink black pop better. No, I don't quite know what they mean by that either. What did you say your name was?"

"It's Stan," says Stan. He takes a swig of the black pop. Seabrook's right. It is delicious.

"Now, let's have the chinwag," says Seabrook. "It's a lovely day, isn't it, Stan?"

"It is," says Stan.

"Though there was a bit of a chill last Wednesday," adds Seabrook.

"Was there?" says Stan.

"There was. But not like that cold snap back in March. And kids today, eh? I mean, it's serious, isn't it? Every time you turn on the telly, there's another one. The world's going to rack and ruin. And the economy! The *economy*! I mean, where's it all going to end?"

Stan swigs the black pop: a strange taste, like blackberries and sardines at the same time. "I don't know," he admits.

"Me neither, Stan. I mean, I was saying to Macintosh just last night—you know, he's the one who married that lass from Pembroke, the one with the bit of a limp after she fell off her bike when she was three—I mean, I was saying to him, 'What's to *become* of us? Where's it going to *end*?' He didn't have a clue, of course. Not surprising when you think what he's been through with that poor dog of his. But I mean, there *is* no answer, is there? I mean, you listen to them talk, and they talk like they know what they're talking about and what they're going to do about it all, and you know they haven't got a clue. I mean, it's like they talk for the sake of talking. Do you know what I mean? And the litter, Stan! It's not like in our day, is it? I blame the teachers. Rack and ruin. And it *is* a long way to Tipperary, that's what folk fail to understand. You've got to look on the bright side, haven't you? There's a light at the end of the . . . But listen, it's been really lovely talking to you, Stan, but I'm afraid I haven't got all day; and anyway, what's it all got to do with the price of fish?"

"I don't know, Mr. Seabrook."

"Exactly! Now. Are you after A, B, C, or D?" He sees Stan's blank expression. "Do you want Golden Greats, Top Notchers, Not Too Bads, or Little Runts?" He sees Stan's continued blank expression. "Tell you what. Come and look at the ponds and I'll explain."

Seabrook leads Stan round the desk to the ponds. He explains that the Golden Greats in Pond A are best of all and most expensive of all, and the Little Runts in Pond D are scrawniest and cheapest. Stan looks down. They are all beautiful to his eyes, the gorgeously curving Golden Greats, the twitchy Little Runts, and all the others in between.

"They're lovely," says Stan. "Each and every one of them."

As if they hear, several fish rise to the surface and turn their eyes and mouths to Stan.

"I'm impressed," says Seabrook. "You've got the touch. I could do you a mixture if you like. How many you after?"

"Half a shoal."

"And who they for?"

"Wilfred Dostoyevsky."

"Aha!" says Seabrook. "Dostoyevsky. A long-time customer of mine." He goes back to the desk and opens a file. "As I thought," he says. "Wilfred Dostoyevsky's custom is to take the Little Runts."

Stan nods. He's already guessed that. The thirteen fish he saved on his birthday were obviously from Pond D.

"But," says Seabrook, "I've heard he's a changed man these days."

"A changed man?"

"News travels fast in the fair, Stan. The story is he's come across some kid who's had an influence on him." He closes the file and peers at Stan. "*Is* he a changed man, Stan?"

"I don't know. I didn't know him before."

"Before he came across *you,* you mean?"

"I don't know," says Stan.

Seabrook smiles. He winks. "It's a pleasure and an honour to have you here, Stan," he says. "Tell you what. I'll do you a mixed half shoal. OK?"

"OK," says Stan.

Seabrook takes his net, dips it into all four ponds, lifts out fish from each, and tips them gently into a plastic carrier filled with clear water. The fish swarm together, becoming accustomed to their new space, then as Stan and Seabrook watch they separate again into As, Bs, Cs, and Ds.

"Funny how that always happens," says Seabrook. He grins. "*Look* at those Golden Greats. *Look* at how splendid they are in there! Don't you think they're splendid, Stan?"

"Yes," says Stan.

"But which are truly your favourites, Stan?"

Stan gazes into the water. "The Little Runts," he says after a moment.

Seabrook grins again. "Thought so. Maybe because you came from the same pond, eh, Stan?" Seabrook smiles.

Stan digs into his pocket and takes out some money. "How much are they?" he asks.

Seabrook takes a few coins from his hand. "That'll do," he says. "Now turn round and I'll get this on your back."

He lifts the plastic water carrier, which has straps hanging from it. He puts the straps over Stan's shoulders. The carrier is heavy, but it settles easily onto Stan's back. Stan feels it hanging there, so close. He thinks he can feel the vibrations of the fish as they swim.

"Feels OK?" asks Seabrook. Stan nods. "Off you go then, Stan." He touches Stan's shoulder. "You know what? The little troubled runts are often the ones that turn out to be best of all."

Stan says good-bye. He walks away, past the empty cages. He's forgotten about the scorpions and the eagle. He feels the vibration of swimming fish at his back. The water carrier glitters and glows.

TWENTY-FOUR

Stan isn't aware of passing through the wall of the tent, but suddenly there he is, out in the fair again. He walks homeward, past the Wild Boar Cookhouse, towards Dostoyevsky. A few kids gather behind him and follow. They poke at the water carrier, point at the fish. They ask if they can have one and Stan laughs and says they'll have to come to Dostoyevsky's hook-a-duck and win one.

"There's a prize every time at Dostoyevsky's!" he says, pleased with himself for advertising the stall so well.

The kids say they will and Stan sees how happy and friendly they are, and with every step he feels more at home. But he also has the feeling of being watched again. He pauses by the wrestling booth and looks around. There's a man standing beside it in the shade.

The kids gasp.

"It's Pancho!" one whispers.

"It isn't. It can't be!"

"It is. I seen him last year in Marrakesh."

"It's Pancho!"

"It's Pancho Pirelli."

The kids quieten down, and Stan senses their trembling and excitement as Pancho comes out from the shade and walks towards them. He's dark-skinned, dark-eyed. Dressed in blue. He heads straight to Stan.

"You're Stan," he says. His voice is soft, foreign, watery. "I've been waiting for you, Stan. All these years I knew there'd be somebody like you and now here you are."

He holds his hand out. Stan takes it. It's odd, but he feels like he's known Pancho for a long, long time.

"I have been watching you," says Pancho. "You are the goldfish boy. Will you come to see me do my act?"

"Yes, but . . ."

"I will be easy to find, Stan. Ask anyone. Come tomorrow, see my act and then we will talk some more."

He turns and walks away. The kids breathe easily again.

"Pancho Pirelli," one whispers. "I seen Pancho Pirelli!"

"Why's he been watching you, Stan?"

"I don't know," says Stan. "I don't know any-thing."

"He's the greatest!"

"We thought he was gone."

"My dad said he'd got gobbled up."

"Gobbled up?" gasps Stan.

"Aye. But he obviously ain't. Mebbe he jus' got chewed a bit."

"They say he's gettin' old. They say he will get proper gobbled up if he don't take care."

Stan has so many questions, but the kids scatter, running away to tell their families and friends that they have stood beside the great Pancho Pirelli.

TWENTY-FIVE

Dostoyevsky's delighted with the fish. He says they're a glorious collection. He catches his breath as he says it. "Did ye hear what I said?" he marvels. "A glorious collection! Ye wouldn't've heard Dostoyevsky sayin' such a thing about a bunch of fish a few short days ago. Would ye, Stan?"

Stan shrugs. "No," he admits.

"Ye're a strange one," says Dostoyevsky, peering into Stan's face.

"Me?" says Stan.

"Aye, ye. Ye're havin' quite an influence on me, young Stan." He snaps open a bottle of beer and swigs from it.

The sky glows like a blazing furnace, then it darkens, darkens. Dostoyevsky says that stalls like hook-a-duck don't do too well once darkness falls. They're too tame for the night, he says. People want the bright lights and the excitement of the waltzer. They want to scream and howl on the roller coaster. They want to be horrified in the haunted house and terrified in the Wall of Death.

They want to spin and twist and plummet and soar. They want to binge on greasy burgers and spicy sauces.

Dostoyevsky sits on the step of the caravan. Stan sits with him as the moon appears above the fair, and the lights and music and voices start to fill the night.

Stan tells him about seeing Pancho Pirelli.

"So it's true," murmurs Dostoyevsky. "He's come again."

"What *is* his act?" Stan asks, but Dostoyevsky shakes his head.

"Best to see it for yourself, Stan. You can go tomorrow."

"He talked to me, Mr. Dostoyevsky."

"You're honoured, Stan."

"He said he'd been waiting for me."

"Did he?" Dostoyevsky reaches out and tousles Stan's hair. "I had the same kind of feeling."

"About what?"

"About you, Stan. From the moment I seen you cleaning them ducks then savin' the fish with the river water. Like you'd been sent to me that day. Like you was special." He grins. "Or mebbe I'm jus'

goin' daft, eh?" He grins again. "But like I said," he continues, "ye're a strange one."

They're silent for a while, staring into the moon.

"These is the joys of the travellin' life," says Dostoyevsky.

"What are?" says Stan.

"The simple things like this, young Stan. Things like sittin' on the caravan step in the light of the lovely moon. They say it makes ye mad, ye know. They say ye shouldn't let the moon shine down on you too much."

"I've heard that," says Stan.

"Do you believe it?" asks Dostoyevsky.

Stan shrugs. He doesn't really know what he believes.

"And then there's some," says Dostoyevsky, "that says the moonlight is a good thing. They say that each and every one of us needs a drop of madness in us. D'ye believe *that,* young Stan?"

Stan wonders about this. He wonders about the world. He wonders about himself and the weird things he's experienced, the weird things he's

124

seen. He looks into the sky and into the universe. He imagines it going on forever and forever to the stars, and way beyond the stars, and way beyond the stars beyond the stars, and he knows that his wondering and wondering will never have an end.

"Well?" whispers Dostoyevsky. "Do we all need a drop of madness in us?"

A dog barks somewhere. A woman sings a sweet song that carries on the air despite the wailing of the fairground and the yelling of the fairground-goers.

"Maybe it's in us anyway," says Stan, "whether we want it or not."

Dosyoyevsky nods. He looks at Stan with fondness and respect in his eyes. "That's very wise," he says.

And both of them relax and smile and let the madness of the moon pour down upon them.

TWENTY-SIX

It's deep into the night, and Stan's in his bed but he's wide awake. Beyond the caravan window, the lights of the fair still flicker and flash, and the moon hasn't yet left the sky. The tank of fish is by his bed. It flickers and flashes too, filled with the fish from the goldfish supplier. Stan feels the excitement and joy of the thirteenth fish as it swims among the new ones. *Welcome,* he hears. *Welcome, my companions.* He hears something else, something much sadder, a snuffling, a catching of breath nearby. He listens. It comes from inside the caravan.

"Nitasha," he whispers. "Nitasha?"

There's no answer, but the snuffling goes on. He crawls from his narrow bunk and along the floor to the rear of the caravan where her bed is, behind a plywood screen. He knocks gently.

"Nitasha. Are you all right, Nitasha?"

"Shove off."

The snuffling starts again. There's a few sobs.

"Nitasha."

"Shove off! What's it got te do with you?"

"Can I come in?"

No answer. He pushes the screen and it opens. He crawls into her tiny compartment.

"What's wrong?" he whispers.

Nitasha pulls the blankets right over her, then she slowly tugs them down so that only her mouth and her nose are visible.

"She *was* lovely," she whispers.

"I bet she was."

"But she didn't *love* me."

"I'm sure she did."

"Why would she go away if she *loved* me?"

"I don't know," whispers Stan, but he knows that he too has left people he loves.

Nitasha tugs the blankets down a bit more. Stan sees her eyes staring out at him.

"Everything's horrible," she says.

"It isn't," he says. "Or it doesn't need to be." He looks away. He's hopeless. He knows nothing. How can he help Nitasha when he's just a kid himself?

"You've got your dad," he whispers at last.

"Him? He can't stand me. He loves *you* more than he loves *me*."

"No, he doesn't," says Stan.

"He wishes *you* were his kid and not *me*."

"No, he doesn't."

"And he's right. I used to be nice, but not no more. I'm lazy and ugly and fat and good for nobody and good for nowt. Now leave me alone."

"Maybe you could start doing things," suggests Stan. "You could help with the stall."

"Help with the stall! Huh. I'll have me own stall one day and I won't need him and I won't need her and I won't need you and I won't need nobody never no more."

"What do you mean, your own stall?"

"I'm gonna get uglier and uglier and horribler and horribler and fatter and fatter and I'm gonna grow a beard and build a stall and I'll be the Ugliest Fattest Bearded Lady You Ever Seen."

"Oh, Nitasha!" says Stan.

"Oh, Nitasha *what*?"

"Oh, Nitasha, you could be lovely. Last night by the fire you started to look really—"

"That's me plan," says Nitasha. "I'll be a freak. I'll make a mint. Then I'll not need nobody."

"Oh, Nitasha!"

"Oh, Nitasha nowt. Now go away." And she pulls

the blankets right over herself again.

Stan turns to leave, starts the crawl back to his bunk. "I'm going to see Pancho Pirelli tomorrow," he says over his shoulder.

"Wow!" she sneers from beneath the blankets.

"You could come with me."

"So people can see your freak at your side?"

Stan hesitates. "No," he says. "So people can see somebody who's nearly like my sister at my side."

Nitasha raises the blankets and stares at him. "Ye're mental," she says. "Stop being stupid. Get back to bed."

Stan crawls back along the caravan floor and climbs into his narrow bunk. He looks across at Dostoyevsky. The man's eyes are open and shining with tears in the moonlight. There's a sob, and then silence, then much later a little whisper from Nitasha.

"Did ye really mean that, Stan?"

"Mean what?"

"About bein' like a sister?"

"Course I did," says Stan.

Then there's silence again, but for the final screams and laughter and wailing from the fair outside.

TWENTY-SEVEN

Stan's excited when he wakes up. It's almost like his birthday's come again. It's a bright clear morning. He helps Dostoyevsky to put up the stall, to set the ducks on the water, to hang up the goldfish in their plastic bags. He goes to the caravan door a couple of times and calls for Nitasha, but there's no answer except a grunt or two.

Dostoyevsky puts his arm round Stan's shoulder. "Leave her, son," he says. "It's how she is. Go on. You jus' go on yer own."

Stan shrugs. He sighs. He's about to set off alone, just like he did on his birthday a few short days ago, but then the caravan door opens and Nitasha's standing there, pink-faced and shy. She's wearing a flowery frock. She's washed her face. She's brushed her hair.

"Nitasha!" says her father in amazement.

She can't look at him.

"You look lovely, love," he says.

He digs into his pocket, finds some cash, shoves it into her hand. Stan sees tears shining in his eyes.

"Go on, love," Dostoyevsky says. "Have a . . ."

"Good time," whispers Stan.

"Good time," says Dostoyevsky.

"Say thank you," whispers Stan to Nitasha.

"Thank you," she murmurs. She raises her eyes for a moment. "Thank you, Dad."

Stan's so pleased and so proud. Nitasha walks at his side into the heart of the fair. They pass the dodgems and the wrestling booth. The boar man at the Wild Boar Cookhouse snarls a smile at them.

"Got yerself a girlfriend, have ye?" he growls.

Stan ignores him and peers towards the trees. It's strange. Today the tent looks just like a painted tent. Its canvas walls are flapping in the breeze, and trees that yesterday looked like real trees are just trees that have been painted on. The paintings are clumsy, like a kid's done them, and the paint's flaking and cracked. And there's a painted sign:

SUPPLY TENT
GOLDFISH, SCORPIONS, EAGLES
AND OTHER SUCHLIKE STUFF
COME INSIDE
WOTCH YER STEP AND YER HEAD!

"Why ain't ye whistlin'?" snarls the boar man.

Stan says nothing.

"Cat got yer tongue?"

Stan says nothing.

"Have ye heard the tale about the man that et the boar?" says the boar man.

"Yes!" says Stan.

"Aha! Then have ye heard the tale about the world that turned into a tent?"

"No," says Stan.

"It ended up lookin' jus' like a tent!" The boar man snuffles with laughter.

The tent door flaps open, and Mr. Smith comes hurrying out. "Are you back for more fish *already*?" he asks.

"No," says Stan.

"You're looking at the tent, aren't you?"

"Yes," says Stan.

"And you think it looks just like a tent, don't you?"

"Yes," says Stan.

"Of course it does!" says Mr. Smith. "If it's a tent, which it is, what else would it look like?"

"I don't know," says Stan.

Mr. Smith looks at his watch. "Listen," he says.

"The tent looked like it did yesterday because yesterday was yesterday. Some days we see more . . . *intensely* than we do on other days. Do you understand?"

"No," says Stan.

"No," says Nitasha.

Mr. Smith ponders. He looks at his watch again. "Nor do I," he admits. "Now, move aside. I am off to see the splendid Pancho Pirelli. Along with many others, as you see."

And Stan turns, and sees that there are many people all hurrying in the same direction. Mr. Smith rushes to join them, and Stan and Nitasha do as well.

3.

THE PIRANHA TANK

TWENTY-EIGHT

So here we are. This is the scene. There's a clearing at the heart of the fair. A grassy space where people are gathering. They've brought picnics, flasks of coffee, crates of beer, bottles of wine. There are a few fires burning and the smell of chops sizzling and spuds baking. Kids wrestle, run, and dance. Babies gurgle and cry.

Nitasha stays close to Stan. They weave their way through the crowd towards a blue trailer. The blue trailer's wrapped in blue tarpaulin, and a huge name is written there in gold:

! PANCHO PIRELLI !

A few people speak to the pair as they pass by. "Hello, young Stan." "How do, Nitasha."

Stan hardly hears them. His eyes are on the trailer, on Pancho's name. He takes Nitasha's hand and leads her forward. He feels like he's been drawn to this place. He shivers with excitement and fear and holds Nitasha's hand tight. "Come on," he whispers to her. "Stay with me, please, Nitasha."

She whispers that she will.

Then there's a hush, and suddenly there's Pancho himself, standing beside the trailer. He's wearing a blue cape that's fastened at his throat with a golden cord. There is a pair of blue goggles on his head. He looks into the crowd and sees Stan there and he smiles, and the smile makes Stan even more excited. Stan leads Nitasha closer, to the front of the crowd, so close they could almost reach out and touch Pancho Pirelli

"Welcome," murmurs Pancho, then his face hardens as he turns his eyes to the crowd "My name," he says into the hush, "is Pancho Pirelli."

People giggle, sigh, and smile.

Pancho raises his hand. "I am here," he says, "to touch the teeth of death for you. I am here to look into its eyes for you. I am here to dance with it for you."

"Do it, Pancho!" someone cries from within the crowd. And other voices start yelling.

"Do it, Pancho!" "Yes! We love you, Pancho!"

"You're a madman, Pancho! You're crazy!" "You're barmy!" "You're wonderful!" "Do it for us, Pancho Pirelli!"

Pancho lets the voices go on for a moment, then he reaches up to the blue tarpaulin that's wrapped around the trailer. He tugs, and the tarpaulin separates like curtains on a stage. And Stan's jaw drops open, for there, behind the tarpaulin, is clear water. The sun's shining down on it, and there's a shoal of fish swimming elegantly in it.

The whole trailer is a fish tank. And the fish inside?

"Piranhas!" gasp the crowd.

"Pancho Pirelli's Perilous Piranhas!"

Pancho turns. The voices fade.

"These," he says, "are my piranhas."

The fish are rather pretty, oval-shaped, silvery-grey, a flush of red on their cheeks and lower jaws. Each one is about the size of a child's head. No bigger than that. Stan stares. "Piranhas!" he whispers to Nitasha. He knows, as most people do, their fierce reputation. These are the lethal fish of myth and legend, the fish that will strip a man to the bone in seconds.

But *these* fish, they seem so tame, so calm. Can they *really* be piranhas?

"*They* aren't piranhas!" somebody yells. "They can't *possibly* be piranhas!"

Pancho smiles. "No," he says. "Of *course* they can't possibly be piranhas. Would you like to dip your hand into the tank to test them out?" He walks forward and mingles with the crowd. "How about you, madam?" he asks. "Or you, sir?"

People laugh. They back away and separate to let Pancho through. Stan watches Pancho weaving his way through the crowd. He watches the fish suspended above so beautifully in their crystal clear water, with their fins and tails propelling them elegantly forward, their mouths opening and closing as if they're saying o O O O O O O o.

"Or you, young sir?" comes the voice from his side.

It is Pancho, of course, leaning down to Stan.

"You look like you know the world of fish," says Pancho. "You look like you could almost be a fish yourself. Would you like to—"

But then he suddenly turns away and reaches out to grab a little boy standing close by, a boy who's eating a sandwich. "Or *you!*" he snaps. "You look like a mischievous kind of boy. Am I right?"

The boy can't speak, but the man with him says, "Aye, you're right, Mr. Pirelli! He *is* a mischievous kind of lad!"

"Daddy!" cries the boy. He tries to pull away from Pancho, but he can't. He gasps and giggles and groans at Pancho's side.

"He's a little monster, Mr. Pirelli!" says the father, who can hardly speak for laughing. "He's a total terror. Me and the missus has often said he should get fed to Pancho Pirelli's piranhas!"

"Then let us *do it!*" says Pancho. He leads the boy towards the tank and takes the sandwich from his hand. "What is *this*?" he asks.

"A . . . a . . . a sossij samwich," stutters the boy.

Pancho holds the sandwich up to the glass walls of the tank. The fish rush furiously towards it. Their jaws open and shut and their eyes glare viciously out through the glass.

"The poor ickle fish are hungry, little boy," says Pancho. "Shall I feed them your sossij samwich?"

"Aye, Mr. Pirelli," whispers the boy.

There's a ladder fixed to the side of the tank. Pancho steps onto it, holding the sandwich in his hand. The fish inside swim upwards as Pancho climbs. The crowd laughs as the boy runs back to his dad. Pancho reaches the top of the ladder. He leans over the tank. He smiles and lets the sandwich fall, and his terrifying fish rush to it and savage it, and there is tumult in the tank, and silence in the crowd.

Stan's heart thunders. He's never seen anything so wild—and all for the sake of a sausage sandwich. What, he wonders, would those piranhas do to a *boy*?

TWENTY-NINE

Pancho smiles. The sandwich has gone. The fish swim with a new energy and urgency, as if they're hunting for something more to gobble up inside that empty tank.

"See?" he says. "See what my fish can do to a sossij samwich. Imagine what they could do to a . . ." He groans in disappointment. "But where is my mischievous boy, my ickle monster? Ah, I see he has runned back to his dada." Pancho frowns. "Give him back! The fish are hungry! They're waiting!"

The boy's father has both arms around his son. He glares at Pancho now, defying him to take the boy.

Pancho relaxes and smiles. "Don't worry, sir," he says. "It's just my little joke. Your monster is safe. Now, watch."

He reaches under the tank and takes out a dead chicken. It has been plucked. He holds it by a leg and lets it dangle in front of him. "It's time for something a little larger," he says to the crowd.

He climbs the ladder again. He lowers the

chicken into the tank. The fish launch themselves at it, and within seconds it has been stripped to the bone. Within a few seconds more, the bone has been stripped to nothing at all. The fish swim on, in circles, in spirals, in threatening figures of eight.

"Do you think they've had enough?" asks Pancho Pirelli.

Down the ladder he comes again. He picks up an old shoe that has been lying on the ground. It's a twisted stiff dark leather thing. It's probably been lying there for months, for years. Pancho weighs it in his palm. He twists it. He pretends to sniff it. The crowd giggles. Then Pancho lobs it upwards, and it curves through the air and lands with a splash in the tank. Straight away it's gone, ripped by the piranhas' teeth, snapped by their jaws, gulped down into their guts. And still they roam, looking for more.

Pancho turns his eyes to Stan, and when he speaks, it's like he's speaking just to him. "Who would dare to dive into this tank, to swim with these fish?" His gaze intensifies. "You? *You?*"

Stan grips Nitasha's hand. He shakes his head. *"No,"* he murmurs. *"No!"*

Pancho moves through the crowd again. "Would you like to see Pancho Pirelli enter the tank?" he asks. "Would you dare to watch if he did? Or would you close your eyes? Would you turn away? Would you run off screaming?"

He holds out a red velvet bag.

"You must pay, of course," he says softly. "You must give money to see a man face such danger." Coins are dropped into the bag. "Thank you, sir," he murmurs. "Thank you, madam." Sometimes he stops and looks at people with sadness or scorn.

"Is that all you're going to give?" he whispers. "Would *you* face death for that? Pay more. Pay *more*! Thank you. Much better." He shakes the bag, jingles the coins. He seeks out those who try to hide, to avoid his gaze, to pay nothing. "I *see* you," he says. "You can't fool *me*. There's no hiding from Pancho Pirelli. You have nothing? Oh, but you must have the tiniest of coins somewhere. A cent, a farthing. Take it out, drop it in, and you will see the greatest act you've ever seen. Thank you, madam. Thank you, sir."

At last he smiles. He carries the heavy bag of coins to Stan. "Will you look after this for me until I return?" he says.

"Yes," says Stan, and takes it from him.

Pancho unties the cord at his throat. The cloak falls from his shoulders. He's wearing blue swimming trunks. He holds the cloak out to Stan. "And this as well?" he asks.

Stan takes the cloak. Pancho climbs the ladder. He pulls his goggles down over his eyes. He leans over the edge of the tank. And in he goes

THIRTY

People clap their hands across their eyes, turn their faces away. They gasp in horror. They imagine the tank turning red with Pancho's blood. There are giggles and laughter and screams. But not from Stan. Yes, his heart thumps, his skin crawls, his hands tremble, but he sees the courage and the beauty of it all. He sees Pirelli dive elegantly down through the water. The fish part to let him in. They arrange themselves around him as he hangs at the centre of the tank, beating the water with gentle movements of his feet and his hands. Pirelli faces outwards, towards the watching crowd, and the fish do the same; and for a moment, everything inside the tank is almost still. Then Pancho moves, a gentle swaying of his body. He tilts his head; he moves his hands; he lifts his feet.

"He's *dancing*!" whispers Nitasha.

And it's true. He dances, and the fish start to dance in formation around him, turning and curving through the water that just a few moments ago was the scene of such savagery.

Then somebody yells out, "Breathe, Pirelli! Breathe!"

And everyone, entranced until now, realizes that Pirelli hasn't taken a single breath since he entered the water. How can he do such a thing? How can he have such control? Surely he must drown. But Pancho's face is calm and his movements are fluid. The crowd pushes closer. They look upwards to the man and the fish dancing before and above them. How does he still live? How do his fish

not strip him to the bone? As if to reassure them, Pirelli rises for a moment to the surface, tilts his face into the air, breathes in, and then dives down again to be with his piranhas. And they dance again, spiralling and turning, performing loops and whirls and somersaults, as if to some beautiful watery music that no one outside the tank can hear.

Then Pancho Pirelli rises. He lifts himself from the water. He climbs out onto the ladder. He raises an arm to acknowledge the wild cheering of the crowd. And then down he comes and takes his cloak from Stan.

"Did you think I would die?" he asks.

"No," whispers Stan.

Pancho smiles and draws the cloak around himself. He lifts the goggles from his eyes. "Do you think *you* will die?"

"Me?" says Stan.

"Yes, you," says Pancho. "Do you think you will die when *your* turn comes to dive into the tank with my piranhas?"

He reaches out and rests a hand on Stan's shoulder. "I will train you well, Stan. I will give you all the help you need. But in the end it will not be about training or help. It's your destiny, Stan. I knew it as soon as I looked at you. You have come to this place to take on the burden of Pancho Pirelli. You will be like me, Stan. You will be a performer of myth and legend. Your name will be written in gold on a blue tarpaulin. Imagine it, Stan."

Stan imagines it:

! STANLEY POTTS !

Then he runs in fear from his fate.

THIRTY-ONE

That night, as the moon shines through the caravan window, Stan sleeps with his hand dangling into the goldfish tank. He feels little fins and little tails rippling against his skin. He dreams of jaws and vicious teeth. He dreams of dancing to weird watery music. Behind her screen, Nitasha can't sleep. She feels like she'll never sleep again. She stares into the moon and listens to the music from a waltzer and feels like she's waking from a sleep that's lasted forever and a day. Dostoyevsky snores, turning and turning in his own narrow bed. His dreams are of Siberia, of blizzards that howl and ice that turns the earth as hard as steel. He dreams of a slender woman dancing on a frozen lake of ice with tiny fragments of frost sparkling in the air around her. And he dreams of his Nitasha. In his dream she, too, is in a world of ice and frost, a world so cold that the girl has turned to ice herself. But there is a glimmer on the horizon, a hint of dawn. Maybe it means that the sun will return and his Nitasha will start to thaw, will start to live again.

But, reader, let's leave this trio for a moment in their caravan. Let's have something like our own dream. Let's rise through the caravan roof and over this strange field filled with sideshows and rides and peculiar practices and magical moments and fires and chops and spuds and scorpions and fish and tents. Let's rise into the moonlight so that the fires shrink to the size of fireflies; the spinning waltzer becomes like a distant comet. Let's rise so that the town that contains the fairground is shrinking too, so that we can see the glistening vastness of the dark sea nearby, and the huge bulges and jagged tops of the mountains. Let's rise towards the moon and the stars and the wonderful and terrifying hugeness of the universe. And let's look down, almost as if we were the moon itself, and see if we can see what has happened to the other fragments of our story.

Look. There's the road between the mountains and the sea that Stan and Dostoyevsky and Nitasha followed in their journey from Fish Quay Lane. Let's follow it back the other way. Look, there's Fish Quay Lane itself, so far off, near the abandoned shipyard. Let's travel through the night and move closer to that place. How can we do this? you may well ask. But it's easy, isn't it? All it takes is a few words put into a few sentences, and a bit of imagination. We could go anywhere with words and our imaginations. We could leave this story altogether, in fact, and find some other story in some other part of the world, and start telling that one. But no. Maybe later. It's best not to leave our story scattered into fragments, so let's find them and start to gather them up.

Aha! Look there, down on the road leading from Fish Quay Lane. See them? Two tattered figures stumbling through the moonlight with sacks on their backs. Let's go closer. It's a woman and a man. Are we surprised to see that this is Annie and Ernie, the evicted relatives of Stanley Potts? They seem to have hardly anything with them, just a few belongings tied up into bundles.

Let's go closer still. What's that in their eyes? Sadness, yes, but determination too—surely it's the determination to find their lost boy and bring him back into their fold. Perhaps they have heard a story of such a boy working on a hook-a-duck stall on a piece of waste ground in a not-too-faraway town. Perhaps they . . . But how can we know what they know and what they think? Can we enter their minds with words and our imaginations? Perhaps we can. But listen, we don't need to. They're speaking.

"We'll find our Stan," says Annie to Ernie.

"Aye, we will!" says Ernie to his wife.

And the two of them step onwards through the night that is already turning into dawn.

There we are, then. They're heading in the right direction. Maybe it won't be long before they're right back where they should be: at the heart of the story.

Keep going, Annie. Keep going, Ernie. The story's waiting for you. Your boy's waiting for you!

Ha! See how they lift their thumbs when the early traffic passes. They're hitchhiking, reader. Let's hope a friendly driver takes them in and carries them fast towards the fair.

But what's this now, clattering along the road in the predawn dark? Oh, heck, it's the DAFT van. And is that Clarence P. Clapp inside it, his hands on the wheel? Is that Doug and Alf and Fred and Ted squashed in beside him? Yes, it is. Their expressions are urgent and determined too. The engine of the DAFT van roars. Its wheels rattle and rumble. Does Clarence P. recognize the two hitch-hikers at the side of the road? Perhaps he does. He slows the van to a walking pace as he passes Annie and Ernie, as if he's about to offer them a lift, but of course he's only teasing. Their faces brighten, then darken as they recognize the van. They lower their thumbs; they look away. Clarence P. Clapp winds down the window, and along with Doug and Alf and Fred and Ted, he hurls a volley of abuse into their ears. Then there's a din of laughter, and the DAFT van's gone, hurtling towards Stan, hurtling back into the tale.

THIRTY-TWO

Stan wakes from his watery dreams. Sunlight's streaming through the caravan window. There are angry voices outside—Dostoyevsky's and Pirelli's. Stan slips out of bed and listens at the door.

"Ye can't jus' come and take him away like that," says Dostoyevsky.

"It is his destiny, sir!" answers Pirelli.

"Destiny! He's got a good life here, and a good home, and a good job!"

"A good job? Looking after a hook-a-duck stall, washing ducks, playing with tiddlers—"

"*Tiddlers?* I'll have ye know that some of these is Golden Greats!"

"*Golden Greats!* Piranhas are the fish that truly matter. Piranhas and nothing else!"

"*Piranhas!* Do you think I'm givin' him to you to get gobbled up by them monsters?"

"Have I been gobbled up, in all my years of performing?"

"But *you* are Pancho Pirelli!"

"And *he* is Stanley Potts! He has the touch; he

has the *magic*. I am certain of it. He will be my apprentice; I will train him and advise him. I will take him to the ancestral home of all piranhas—to the Amazon, the Orinoco, the great rivers of South America. In those far-off and wonderful places he will learn to swim with piranhas, to think like piranhas, to feel like piranhas. And then . . ."

"And then what?"

"And then, Mr. Dostoyevsky, he will return in glory. He will perform for us all. He will become as great and as famous as the great Pancho Pirelli himself! As with all of the great fairground performers through history—as with the legendary Houdini himself!—he will become a boy of myth." Pirelli speaks more softly. "Surely you yourself have seen, sir, that there is something special about this boy."

"Of course I have," says Dostoyevsky.

"And surely," continues Pirelli, "you do not think that he arrived in this place by chance."

"Of course I don't," says Dostoyevsky. "Right from the start I knew there was somethin' special about the lad."

"Well, then!"

"But I thought his specialness was to do with goldfish, with hook-a-duck, with—"

"He has a greater calling, Mr. Dostoyevsky. He is called to be no less than the next Pancho Pirelli."

There's silence between the men. Stan gets ready to come out of the caravan.

"But, Mr. Pirelli," says Dostoyevsky, "we've come to love the lad. He's one of the family!"

Stan twists the handle, opens the door, steps outside. Both men turn to him.

"Sir," says Pancho softly. "There are greater callings, even, than family."

"*Are* there? *Are* there?"

These words are spoken by Nitasha. She steps out of the caravan just after Stan, pulling a dressing gown around her. She stamps her feet.

"Who do ye think ye *are,* talkin' about our Stan like that? Oh aye, I know you're the great and marvellous and famously wonderful and stunningly spectacular Pancho precious Pirelli. But what makes you think you can talk about Stan like he's a slave or somethin', like he's got no choice or somethin'?"

Dostoyevsky looks at his daughter in amazement. "Well said, Nitasha," he mutters.

"Huh!" she answers. "Never mind yer 'Well said, Nitashas'. You're just as bad as him. Clean them ducks, fill that pool, watch that stall, buy them fish! Oh, Stan, you're so *special*. Oh, Stan, we love you *so* much. But what choice does he have in the matter, eh? The poor lad dun't know if he's comin' or goin'. Do you, Stan?"

"Pardon?" says Stan.

"You don't know if you're comin' or goin', *do* you? No, you don't. If Stan had *his* way—and I don't know why he *hasn't*—he'd be back home safe and sound at . . . What's it called, Stan?"

"Fish Quay Lane," says Stan.

"Exactly!" says Nitasha. "He'd be back home in Fish Quay Lane. But, oh no. It's clean them ducks, fill that pool, buy them bloomin' fish—"

"Shh," says Stan.

"Eh?" says Nitasha.

"Be quiet."

"I'm jus' tellin' them they got to ask you what *you* want, Stan."

"I know that," says Stan.

"So what *do* you want?"

Stan sighs. "I want my breakfast."

"Your breakfast?" says Dostoyevsky.

"Yes. I want hot chocolate and toast and I want to sit at a table and eat it properly like I haven't done since a long, long time ago."

"Right," says Dostoyevsky.

"Right," says Pirelli.

"And I want you all to be quiet and to stop arguing while I eat it," adds Stan.

"OK," says Dostoyevsky. "Breakfast. There'll be a supplier for that, I s'pose. Do ye want to help me find it, Mr. Pirelli?"

Pancho looks at Stan. "Would you like me to?" he says.

"Yes!" says Stan.

And the two men head off towards the heart of the fair.

THIRTY-THRee

"Men!" says Nitasha. She sits down on the caravan step. "Do you *want* to be the next Pancho Pirelli?" she asks Stan.

Stan shrugs. "Dunno. I've never really wanted *anything* very much."

"It looks very *dangerous*."

"That's true. But when I saw Mr. Pirelli swimming with the piranhas, I kind of knew I could too."

"Did you?"

"Yes. I was scared, but I kind of know what it feels like to be Mr. Pirelli. And I kind of know what it feels like to be a fish."

"*What?*" exclaims Nitasha.

"I know. It sounds mad. But I do."

Nitasha laughs. She walks over to Stan and lifts the collar of his shirt and looks down at his back.

"What you doing?" asks Stan.

"Lookin' for your fins," she says.

Stan laughs. He pops his mouth open and closed: *O O O O.*

"Anyway," he says, "you were wrong. I don't

really want to go back home to Fish Quay Lane. I think I'd quite like to see the Amazon and the Orinoco. That'd make a change. But there's other things I need to sort out first."

"Like your aunt and uncle," says Nitasha.

"Yes," says Stan.

Nitasha sighs. "I'm sorry I was so horrible," she says.

"That's OK."

"No, it's not. I'm really sorry. Do you think they'll look for you?"

"Eh?" says Stan.

"Do you think they'll miss you and come lookin' for you?"

Stan shrugs. "Dunno," he says. He thinks of Ernie, of how weird he became. Maybe he's become even weirder.

"Did they love you?" asks Nitasha.

"Oh yes," says Stan.

"So they'll come lookin' for you. And mebbe find you."

"Maybe. But when they find me, they'll find a different Stan from the one they think they're looking for."

Nitasha grins. "They'll find a Stan that's a bit more like a fish."

"Yes," says Stan, and for a moment he thinks about Annie and Ernie, and he hopes they're missing him now; he hopes they're searching for him.

Then he looks at Nitasha again. She's so different today. She's another one who's changing. "What do *you* want to be?" he asks.

She laughs. "The Ugliest Fattest Bearded Lady You Ever Seen!" she says.

"You don't mean that, Nitasha."

"I did yesterday."

"But not today."

"No. Something's changed."

"Maybe," says Stan, "we can all be something special if we put our minds to it."

"Mebbe," says Nitasha. "But like you, I've got other things to sort out first. And what I really want is for me mum to come back home from Siberia."

"And maybe she will."

"Mebbe she will. Oh, look!" Nitasha points to Dostoyevsky and Pirelli, who are coming towards the caravan carrying a table full of breakfast.

"Toast, hot chocolate, marmalade, butter, and fresh orange juice," says Pirelli.

They all sit and eat. The sun shines down on them. The food and drink are delicious. After a time, Stan turns to Dostoyevsky.

"Mr. Dostoyevsky," he says. "I don't want to stop working at the hook-a-duck stall. But I think I *would* like to try swimming with piranhas."

"Would you, lad?"

"Yes," says Stan.

And Mr. Dostoyevsky looks into Stan's eyes and says, "Mebbe I'm wrong to stand in the way of a boy's destiny." He turns to Pancho Pirelli. "Will you train him well?"

"Of course," says Pancho,

"Then OK," says Dostoyevsky.

THIRTY-FOUR

"Your enemy," says Pirelli, "will not be the piranha. Your enemy will be fear. Do you understand?"

"I think so, Mr. Pirelli," says Stan.

It's later that morning. Pancho Pirelli and Stan have left Dostoyevsky and Nitasha at the hook-a-duck stall. They're standing beside the piranha tank. It's the start of Stan's training.

"Good!" continues Pirelli. "You must not be scared. You must be brave and bold. And you must become Stanley Potts."

"But I *am* Stanley Potts," says Stan.

"You must become *the* Stanley Potts, Stan. You must become the Stanley Potts of myth and legend. Do you understand?"

Stan's not sure if he understands or not. He looks into the tank. The piranhas swim past without glancing at him. He sees their teeth, the way those on the top jaws interlock with those on the bottom, and he can't help shuddering.

"I was a boy once," says Pirelli. "I remember

the first time I saw the piranhas. I remember the first time I entered the water."

"Where was that, Mr. Pirelli?"

Pancho looks at Stan and his eyes go all dreamy. "In the lands of my childhood, Stan. In the distant rainforests of Venezuela and Brazil. I walked as a boy on the banks of the Amazon and the Orinoco, where there are monkeys and snakes and birds as bright as the sun and frogs the colour of flame. I was trained by the mysterious wise men of the rainforest. I spent years there in meditation and training." He looks sideways at Stan. "You too must have an exotic infancy, Stan."

"But I grew up in Fish Quay Lane," says Stan, "with Uncle Ernie and Auntie Annie."

"That means nothing," says Pirelli. "You must *invent* a new infancy, Stan."

"Tell lies, you mean?"

"No. You must . . . create a myth. Come with me. I have things to show you. They will help."

He leads Stan round the tank to a blue camper van. He takes Stan inside. The place is neat and tidy. On the walls are paintings of exotic beasts in exotic jungles, of dazzling fish and dazzling birds. There are photographs of Pirelli standing in front of the piranha tank alongside film stars and princesses and politicians. Stan sits on a wooden chair while Pancho opens a drawer and takes out two photographs.

The first shows a skinny and rather sad-looking boy dressed in shorts and a grey school blazer with a white shirt and striped cap.

"This is me as I was," says Pirelli.

He shows Stan the other, this time a bare-chested boy in blue swimming trunks and a blue cloak who looks bravely out through blue goggles at the camera.

"And this is me as I became."

"In Venezuela?" asks Stan.

"No," says Pirelli. "In Ashby de la Zouch."

"Ashby de la *Zouch*?"

"Yes," says Pirelli. "It's quite close to Birmingham."

"But what about . . ."

"The Orinoco? The Amazon? I have read about them, of course. I have seen photographs and films. They do seem rather marvellous. And yes, it is my intention to go there one day—with you, Stan, I hope—but no, I have never been anywhere near the Amazon. Or the Orinoco."

"So the story of your childhood is . . ."

"Yes, Stan. A story. A legend."

Stan sighs. It's all getting a bit much for him. Maybe he *should* be heading back to Fish Quay Lane.

Pirelli watches him. "I'm only telling you this because I trust you, Stan. I know that you will tell no one. I know that you are true, because when I first saw you I recognized myself."

Pirelli puts a glass of dark liquid into Stan's hand. Stan sniffs it. "This is black pop!" he says.

"That's right. Drink it up. It'll fortify you."

Stan sips, and just like last time he finds it weird and delicious.

"Now I will tell you the true truth," says Pirelli. "I was a rather unhappy and lonely boy. My parents had died when I was a tiddler—"

"Just like mine," says Stan.

"Yes, Stan. As I suspected, just like yours. I was taken on by some far-flung members of the family, a grizzly, miserable pair called Uncle Harry and Aunt Fred."

"Aunt *Fred*?"

"Short for Frudella," explains Pirelli. "Though she *should* have been a man, considering the hair on her, the pipe she smoked, the distance she could spit, and the venom with which she could hit. Anyway, they put me in a school that filled me with hate and dread. St. Blister's, it was called. I'll cut a long story short, Stan. A circus came to town; I ran away to it."

"They never found you?" asks Stan.

Pirelli shrugs. He shakes his head. "I suspect they hardly looked for me."

"Is that when you started to swim with piranhas?"

"No. I mucked out the camels and the llamas. I brushed the zebras and washed the elephants.

Lovely things they were. Then one spring Pedro Perdito arrived."

"Pedro Perdito?"

"And his piranhas. Now, he really *did* come from Brazil. He said he did, anyway. He spotted me just like I spotted you. He said our meeting was destined. He educated me in the ways of fish and of myths. He trained me, and turned me into what I am today, the great and extraordinary Pancho Pirelli. Here he is, look."

Another photograph. It seems ancient, like the colour in it has been painted on. It shows a dark-skinned dark-haired moustached man in a sky-blue cape. Behind him is a piranha tank with the ruddy-jawed fish swimming in it, and on the curtain which has been drawn aside you can see the folded letters of his name.

"Pedro Perdito!" says Pancho. "A man of wonder. A man of miracles. Pedro Perdito, my master. Isn't he marvellous?"

"Yes," says Stan.

"Good. Now, drink your black pop, and put these on."

"Put what on?"

Pirelli grins. He reaches into the drawer again. He takes out a pair of sky-blue trunks and a sky-blue cape and a pair of goggles.

"These!" he says. "The trunks and cape and goggles that Pancho Pirelli wore as a boy. The trunks and cape and goggles that have been waiting for the new Pancho!"

THIRTY-Five

Stan does look rather splendid in his new kit. He's scrawny and skinny, and of course he's still our little Stan, but he already feels like a different *kind* of Stan. He stands beside the piranha tank in the morning sunshine with Pancho. They gaze together at the lethal fish.

"I am not going to throw you straight in, of course," says Pancho.

What? Throw me in! thinks Stan.

"I suppose I should train you up, like Dostoyevsky said," continues Pancho. "It's the modern way, isn't it—education and training, et cetera, et cetera?"

"I suppose so, Mr. Pirelli."

"Then let us begin. First of all you must be educated. Lesson one: getting to know the piranha. Here are some books."

Pirelli searches in the space under the tank. He takes out a couple of battered books: an ancient school encyclopaedia and an ancient atlas. The first tells Stan in

faded print that the piranha is an aggressive flesh-eating fish from the rivers of South America. It says: *Do not enter a river where the piranha is suspected.* The second shows him the routes of the Amazon and the Orinoco through the wilderness of the South American rainforest. It says: *Much of this vast area is still unexplored.*

"You knew those things already, of course," says Pirelli. "By the way, I take it you can swim."

Stan remembers when he used to go to school, the class visits to Fish Quay Swimming Pool— thrashing about in the water with dozens of other kids while the teacher stood in a suit at the side of the pool and yelled at them to behave themselves.

"Yes," he says. "Or at least I used to be able to. I've got my fifty metres badge."

"Good," says Pirelli. "Though this is a different *kind* of swimming. More like controlled sinking, I suppose. We will have to work on your breathing. Hold your breath."

"Sorry?" says Stan.

"Take a deep breath and hold it for as long as you can."

Stan breathes in deeply. He holds it in. Fifteen seconds pass. He feels like he's going to burst. He breathes out loudly and sucks in air again.

"We'll aim to get you up to a minute or so by the end of the week. Can you dance?" asks Pirelli.

Stan has never considered the subject. "I don't know," he admits.

"Neither did I when I was your age. Uncle Harry and Aunt Fred weren't known for their love of dancing. Were *your* aunt and uncle?"

"No," says Stan.

"I thought not. But I imagine that you will find, as I did, that you are a natural. Try a little, please."

"A little what?"

"A little dancing. Just move as if you're dancing underwater to the sound of unheard music. Go on. Don't be shy."

Stan looks around. A small crowd has gathered. Pancho calls to them.

"There will be no performance until this evening! Come back then, please."

A few people move on, but others stay. One of them is Tickle Peter. Stan waves. Peter waves glumly back.

"This is Stanley Potts!" calls Pirelli. "He will become one of the greats!" Then he adds, "His first performance, however, will not be for some time." He turns back to Stan. "Ignore them, Stan. Their time will come. Now show me some dancing."

Stan shuffles his feet a little. He sways his hips. He nods his head up and down.

"We'll work on it," says Pirelli. "Now, the real test. It is time for you to confront the inner piranha."

"The inner piranha?" says Stan.

"You must imagine that the fish are swimming beside you. You must imagine that you are swimming alongside them. You must look into their eyes and show them that you are bold and brave. Can you do that, Stan?"

Stan shrugs. It seems easy enough.

"Close your eyes and do it, Stan," says Pancho. Stan closes his eyes. "See the fins and the scales and the teeth. Feel the fins and tails brushing against your skin. Can you imagine it all, Stan?"

Stan shrugs again. "Yes," he says.

"Excellent. Now look into their eyes, Stan. Be calm and confident."

Stan's good at this. He sees the fish. He feels the

coolness of the water. He sees the teeth. He feels the tails and fins. It's quite pleasant, rather like the dreams he has had of swimming with his goldfish.

"Have they bitten you yet?" asks Pirelli.

"What?" says Stan.

"Have they *bitten* you yet? Is there any blood?"

Stan sighs. Of course they haven't bitten him! "No," he says.

"Excellent! You may open your eyes again."

Stan opens his eyes.

"That was a big success," says Pancho.

"But it was *easy*," says Stan.

"Easy for *you*, perhaps. But you are Stanley Potts. For most people, the inner piranha is as lethal as the outer. The thought of imagining the piranha is almost as terrifying as the thought of entering the tank with it. Here, have some more black pop."

Stan swigs the pop. He looks at the tank. Half a dozen of the piranhas have gathered in a little crowd, close to the edge of the tank, and they're gazing out at him.

Hello, my companions, he murmurs inside himself. *Hello,* he hears back from deep inside himself.

THIRTY-SIX

"Mr. Pirelli," says Stan.

"Yes."

"The training doesn't seem very . . . organized."

"You're right, Stan. It doesn't. Thing is, I've never had an apprentice before. And being *the* Stanley Potts is not really about training. It is about belief. It is about dreams. When you are in your caravan tonight with Mr. Dostoyevsky and Nitasha, I want you to dream of swimming with piranhas. I want you to dream of your childhood by the Orinoco. Can you do that, Stan?"

"Yes," says Stan. "Is this how Pedro Perdito trained you, Mr. Pirelli?"

"Not really," says Pirelli.

"Then how did he train you?"

"He threw me in."

"He threw you in?" cried Stan.

"Yes. He said he was certain that it was my destiny to be the next Pedro Perdito. But he also said there was only one way to be truly certain. So he grabbed me, carried me up the ladder, and in I went."

"And what happened?"

"Nothing. I thrashed around for a few seconds, Pedro watched what was going on, the fish swam happily around me. Then Pedro hauled me out, said I was the right person, gave me some trunks and a cape, and I was off."

Stan stares. He chews his lips at the thought of it.

"It was the old days, Stan," says Pirelli. "It was a different world. We did things differently."

Stan closes his eyes. He sees a boy just like himself thrashing in the water all those years ago.

"Why didn't they eat you, Mr. Pirelli?" he asks. "Why don't they eat you now?"

Pirelli smiles. "That is the question, isn't it?" he says. "It is the one and only question. They do not eat me, because they know I am not there to be eaten. They do not eat me, because I am Pancho Pirelli."

"And they will not eat me, because I am Stanley Potts."

"Correct."

Stan looks at the fish, swimming elegantly through the water. He looks behind him. Tickle Peter peers glumly at the tank. The boar man is there chewing a chop. The lady from the haunted house waves her fangs at him. Further away, he sees Nitasha and Dostoyevsky making their way towards them through the stalls.

"There's another secret as well," adds Pancho.

"What kind of secret?" asks Stan.

"A secret that can only be divulged to those who swim with the piranha."

"People like me?"

"Yes."

"What is it?"

Pancho looks over both shoulders. "You'll tell nobody?" he whispers.

"Nobody," swears Stan.

"OK. The stories about piranhas—about them eating people and stripping them to the bone—well, that's all they are. Just stories."

"So they don't do it?" asks Stan.

"Yes, they do, but not very often. Of course, you can never be certain. Every time I dive in, there's always that little worry: is this the day of doom?"

Stan ponders. "So all that stuff about being *the* Stanley Potts," he says, "and about being a boy of myth and legend, that doesn't really matter?"

"Of course it matters!" cries Pancho. "You are a performer! You must be a hero and draw crowds of admirers to you. And the fish will respond to it. They might not look very clever, but they know a true performer when he turns up in their tank."

The two of them turn to stare at the fish. The fish stare back.

"Mr. Pirelli," says Stan.

"Yes, Stan?"

"Maybe you should throw me in, like Pedro did to you."

"Look at the teeth, Stan," says Pirelli.

"I'm looking," says Stan.

"Remember the chicken, Stan. And the sandwich. And the question: is this the day of doom?"

"I'm remembering. And the shoe. But I just feel that I'll be all right. That maybe the only way to train me properly is to train me like Pedro trained you." Stan looks at the watchers. "It'll be my first performance. I'll pretend I'm terrified."

Pancho Pirelli beams with pleasure. "You are indeed a true performer, Stan. You're a showman."

Stan beams back at Pancho. To his own astonishment, he has to agree that he does feel like a true performer. What on earth would Annie and Ernie make of it all?

"This is the final sign I need," says Pancho.

"What do you mean, the final sign?"

"It shows that you are indeed the next Pancho Pirelli. You do not need to be *trained.* It is the statement of a true swimmer with piranhas: *Throw me in!* Are you ready, Stan?"

Stan steels himself. "Yes," he says.

"I wouldn't do this unless I was pretty sure you'd be safe, you know."

"I know that, Mr. Pirelli."

Pancho turns to the watching crowd. "My friends!" he calls. "This is a historic moment! This is the great and wonderful Stanley Potts, the boy who has a date with destiny! Come closer. Watch him enter the tank of the piranhas. Watch him stare into the face of death! Watch him dance!"

The watchers edge closer.

"But he's just a little lad!" calls someone.

"I too was once a little lad!" responds Pancho. "So were all of us!"

"I wasn't!" yells the woman with the fangs.

"And I was a little boarlet!" snarls the boar man.

Pancho ignores them. He takes hold of Stan's arm and guides him towards the tank. "Are you certain?" he mutters.

Stan takes a deep breath. "Yes, Mr. Pirelli," he says. "Yes."

He pretends to hold back.

"It's cruelty!" comes a voice. "The lad'll get gobbled up!"

The crowd starts to close in.

"Faster, Stan!" whispers Pirelli. He slings Stan across his shoulder. He begins to climb the ladder.

"Somebody stop him!" a man yells.

"I can't look!"

"It's insane!"

"It's criminal!"

"It's murder!"

"STOP!" shouts Stan. "PUT ME DOWN, MR. PIRELLI!"

Pancho stops, lets Stan swing down from his shoulders. Stan climbs the rest of the ladder on his own. He stands there at the top, all alone.

"It's all right, my friends!" he calls. "I won't be eaten! I am Stanley Potts!"

"NO!" yells Nitasha.

"Don't be stupid, lad!" calls the fang woman.

"NO, STAN!" cries Dostoyevsky. "YOU WERE JUS' MEANT TO BE PRACTISIN' TODAY!"

Stan holds up his hand to silence the voices. He feels proud and strong. He pulls the goggles down over his eyes.

"I will not die!" he calls. He stares down into the tank. He sees the waiting piranhas staring back at him. Is that hunger in their eyes?

"NOOOOO!" yells Dostoyevsky.

Stan takes a deep breath. He stands right on the edge of the tank.

"Farewell, my friends!" he calls.

Dostoyevsky leaps past Pirelli, races up the ladder, reaches for Stan. Too late. As Dostoyevsky grabs for him, Stan steps aside, topples forward, and in he goes.

THIRTY-SEVEN

At this point, we could go on another journey to another part of the tale. We could rise from the fairground and seek out the road and see how Annie and Ernie are getting on. We could look down and watch the clattering DAFT van and the barmy men inside. We could travel even further, as far as Siberia, to see if there's any sign of Mrs. Dostoyevsky and her ballerinas, to see if there's any way of bringing her back to her lonely Nitasha. We could even leave this tale altogether and start another. But no. This is probably not the time. This is probably the time to keep focused on our hero, on Stanley Potts, don't you agree?

OK. So in he goes, into the lethal water, the tank of doom, the . . .

Down he goes, head first towards the bottom. The tank becomes a storm of bubbles and splashes, of floundering boy and whirling fish. Stan bounces off the bottom. He looks nothing like a true performer. The fish swirl around him in confusion. He rises to the surface to gulp some air. That's when

Dostoyevsky catches him and hauls him out.

"STAN!" he yells. "YOU'RE S'POSED TO BE JUS' PRACTISIN'!"

"THAT'S WHAT I'M DOING!" Stan yells back. "THROW ME BACK IN!"

Dostoyevsky can't do that, of course. He slings Stan across his shoulder and carries him back down to the ground. Pancho Pirelli comes to stand beside them.

"What you smiling at, Pirelli?" says Dostoyevsky. "The lad could've been killed in there."

"I'm smiling," says Pancho, "because you got him out with perfect timing, Mr. Dostoyevsky. You could almost be part of the act. Would you like to join us?"

"Join you?" yells Dostoyevsky. "This is madness, Pirelli. The lad had hardly heard of a piranha before yesterday, and now you've got him in there swimmin' with them!"

"Yes." Pancho smiles. "Isn't he a wonderful boy? He grew up by the shores of the Orinoco, you know."

"No, he didn't! He grew up in Fish Quay Lane."

"Hush," says Pancho. He raises his voice so that the onlookers can hear. "He grew up by the shores of the Orinoco. He was reared by the wise men of the South American rainforest."

"No, he *wasn't*," says Nitasha, who's joined them.

Now Stanley laughs. "Yes, I was, Nitasha." He winks at her. "I *was*. It's all part of my legend. And I *can* swim with piranhas."

"But you need more practice, lad," says Dostoyevsky. "It's been no time since you were washin' plastic ducks, and now you're swimmin' at the shores of death!"

"OK," says Pancho. "We'll have a bit more practice. Then there'll be a performance that'll go down in history. How about tonight, Stan?"

"Tonight?" says Dostoyevsky.

"Yes," says Stan. "Tonight." He hugs Dostoyevsky and Nitasha. "I'll be prepared. It'll be all right."

"He *is* a special kind of lad," says Pancho. "You said that yourself."

"I did," agrees Dostoyevsky. He gulps.

"Please say yes," begs Stan.

"OK," whispers Dostoyevsky. "Tonight. But lots of practice first!"

Pancho smiles broadly, then turns to the worried watchers.

"This was just a trial run, ladies and gentlemen,"
he announces. "Now spread the word. Tell your
friends. Tonight will be the first public performance
of Stanley Potts. Tonight a star is born!" He widens
his eyes. "Either that, or a star is gobbled up!"

THIRTY-EIGHT

OK. Now's our chance to check what's happening on the road from Fish Quay Lane. Let's head out of the fairground. Let's rise and look down. Oh, heck! There's the DAFT van already heading into town with the DAFT message written on the side and with Clarence P. and Doug and Alf and Fred and Ted bundled up inside. They're approaching the traffic lights. And look, there's that same policeman waiting at the junction. The lights turn red, the policeman strolls into the road and glares in through the windscreen.

"Best behaviour, lads!" warns Clarence P. Clapp. "This is an ossifer of the law come to call."

The policeman reads what is written on the side of the van. He approaches the driver's door. Clarence P. winds the window down.

"Good afternoon, ossifer!" he says. "It is good to know that you is fighting wickedness in this town."

"What is your name?" asks the policeman. "And what is the purpose of your visit?"

"My name," says Clarence P., "is Clarence P.

Clapp, Esquire, and my porpoise is to seek out daftness and destroy it."

"Is it now?" says the policeman.

"It is," says Clarence P. "For I, sir, is a DAFT envistigator."

"Is you now?"

"Aye, ossifer. A envistigator with seven stars, two pips, and a certificate signed by the Chief High Envistigator hisself. I envistigate strange things, peculiar things, things what shouldn't even *be* things. And I bring them to a complete and nutter halt!"

"Do you now?"

"Aye, sir. And these is my lads, Doug and Alf and Fred and Ted. Say hello, lads."

"Hello, ossifer," grunt the lads.

"Hello, lads," says the policeman.

"Could I be bold enough to ask," says Clarence P., "if there is any fishiness or daftness what needs to be envistigated in this here town?"

The policeman leans on the window. "We live in a wicked world, do we not, Mr. Clapp?"

"Indeed we do," agrees Clarence P.

"So there is always fishiness," says the policeman. "There is always daftness. There are always peculiar goings-on. There are always vagabonds and waifs and strays and wicked folk that would lead us all astray. Let me tell you that right now, not one mile from here, we have a field full of—"

At that moment, a car horn sounds. The policeman leans back from the van and glares at the traffic behind.

"Oh sorry, officer!" comes a timid call.

The policeman scribbles something in a notebook and turns back to the van.

"You has a field full of what?" asks Clarence P.

"Of fishiness, Mr. Clapp. A field full of shenanigans and peculiar goings-on."

"That's disgracious," says Doug.

"Appallin'," says Alf.

"Frightful," says Fred.

"Well said, Fred," says Ted.

A car horn sounds again. The policeman leans back a second time and gazes out into the darkening afternoon.

"Would you like my lads to see who is tootin' their hooter and put it to a halt?" asks Clarence P.

"Indeed I would," says the policeman. He moves

aside as the lads clamber out of the van and head towards the cars behind. He smiles. "You are a man after my own heart, Mr. Clapp."

"Us enemies of fishiness must stick together, ossifer," declares Clarence P.

"Indeed we must," agrees the policeman. He points towards the waste ground where the fair is. "Now, if you drive your DAFT van down that lane there, you will find more fishiness than you could ever imagine."

The lads quickly return. They climb proudly back into the van.

"We found the hooter-tooter, ossifer," says Alf.

"And the hooter-tootin' is now over," says Doug.

"Thank you, lads," says the policeman. "Off you go, and see what other daftness you can put an end to." He steps back and salutes as Clarence P. Clapp drives off and heads down the lane towards the fair.

"*That* is a man that is fighting the good fight," says Clarence P. "Now, lads. Eyes peeled for daftness."

THIRTY-NINE

What do you think? Is Stan off his rocker? Has he gone too far? Should he ditch it all—the piranha tank, the cloak and trunks, the thirteenth fish, the hook-a-duck? Should he go back to having an ordinary life? But what's an ordinary life for Stanley Potts? And what would *you* do if somebody came up to you out of the blue and told you there was something very *special* about you? That you had a special talent, a very special skill, and if you dared use it you could become famous; you could become great; you could turn from being *you* into being a very special kind of *you*?

That's the question, isn't it? What if something like the piranha tank appeared in your life? What if somebody like Pancho Pirelli invited you to jump in?

Would you be brave and bold?

Would you face up to your fears?

Would you jump in?

You can't know the answer, can you? Not really. You can't know what you'd do until the very moment when you're standing above the piranha tank and the piranhas are gazing up at you and showing their teeth.

It's nice to wonder, though, isn't it?

So Stan practises all afternoon with Pancho. He practises holding his breath; he practises dancing. He faces his inner piranha time and again. He imagines his exotic childhood by the Amazon and the Orinoco. He imagines the heat and the rain and the burning sun and trees as vast as cathedrals and birds as bright as the sun. He imagines the whispered instructions given by the wise men of the rainforest.

He also spends a little time with Dostoyevsky and Nitasha. They tell him it's the biqqest day of his life. They'll be there watching him, applauding him, praying for him.

"I'm terrified," admits Dostoyevsky, "but I'm dead proud of ye, son. Who'd've known, that mornin' ye turned up at the hook-a-duck stall, what it would all lead to?"

Nitasha smiles. "You make me think that anythin's possible, Stan," she says shyly, and she lifts her eyes to the brightening moon, and Stan knows she's thinking of a slender woman in faraway Siberia.

Stan dips his hand into the fish tank. He feels the fins and tail of the thirteenth fish, the fish he saved, the fish that somehow showed him the special talents inside himself. Then once again he makes his way through the darkening fair towards Pirelli and the piranha tank. People whisper and murmur as he passes by. "That's Stanley Potts. Yes! *The* Stanley Potts." Stan waves to those who call out his name. He blushes at their praise. He grins at their encouragement. His cloak flaps behind him as he walks.

He doesn't see the five men who watch from beside the Wild Boar Cookhouse.

"Aha!" says Clarence P. "Aha-ha-ha-ha-ha!"

It's him, of course. Him and his lads. By now, Clarence P. Clapp and the lads have seen enough fishiness to last them a hundred years. Disgracious fishiness. Appallin' fishiness. They know they've surely come to the land of Rackanruwin.

"Aha-ha-ha-ha-ha-ha-ha!" mutters Clarence P.

"What is it, boss?" says Doug.

"I should of knowed!" says Clarence P. "I should of thunk of it!"

"Thunk of what?" says Ted.

"Thunk of what might be behind all this. Thunk of what might be right at the heart of it!"

"What *is* at the heart of it?" says Ted.

"That!" he answers. "Act natural, now. And look quick where I is looking and where I sees the face of evil."

The lads swivel and look at Stan, whose blue cloak flaps around him as he walks.

"You has seen that face before, lads," says Clarence P. "You might well have forgetted it. But not Clarence P. Clapp, Esquire. Clarence P. remembers everything, always, everywhere. Clarence P. is not one to be tricked or fooled. Remember Fish Quay Lane, lads?"

"Aye, boss," mutter the lads, though Fred and Ted glance at each other and scratch their heads.

"There was a lad there—I say a lad, though I should say a monster—that escaped just before we done the evicshon. And when we looked at him, we was looking upon the face of evil."

"I remember, boss," says Ted. "It was horrible, boss. It was like a nightmare, boss."

"Well said, Ted," says Fred.

"And now the nightmare is back," Clarence P. tells them. "This time it is dressed in a sky-blue cloak."

"Aaarrrgggh!" says Alf.

"Can I smash his face in *now,* boss?" asks Doug.

"No, Doug," says Clarence P. "Can you see how he is loved in this place? Can you hear how these fishy folk think that he is the pea's knees?"

"Aye, boss," answers Doug.

"So we must bite our time. We must wait for our moment. But when we get him we will get him proper. We will rip out the heart of fishiness in this place and put it to an end . . . forever."

Stan reaches the piranha tank.

"Tonight," says Clarence P., "is when all fishiness will come to a complete and nutter end."

FORTY

They watch Stan disappear into Pancho Pirelli's caravan.

"Would you like to eat?" growls the boar man from the counter of the Wild Boar Cookhouse.

"Eat what?" says Clarence P.

"Chops!" growls the boar man. "Or a sausage or three. Or a burger, perhaps."

"What is they made of?" asks Clarence P.

"Best boar, of course," growls the boar man. He leans towards them. "You look like a bunch of upright fellers. You look like fellers that'd benefit from chomping on the boar."

"We certainly is fellers of a different caliper from others what we have seen in this place," agrees Clarence P.

"Then come and eat. There's plenty here for all of you."

Clarence P. and the lads stand at the counter of the Wild Boar Cookhouse. They chomp on the delicious boar meat.

"Is it tasty?" asks the boar man.

"It is delicious," mumbles Alf.

"Is it making you hairy?"

"Hairy?" says Doug.

"Aye! Hairy like a boar. Like in the tale!"

"In what tale?" asks Fred.

"In the tale about the man that et the boar. Shall I tell ye it?"

"No, sir!" says Clarence P. "We is not interested in silly tales. We is interested in truth and facts."

"Then shall I tell ye the *truth* about the man that et the boar?"

"No."

"He turned into a boar hisself," growls the boar man.

"That, sir," says Clarence P., "sounds distinctly like a tale."

"Perhaps it is. Perhaps the truth and the tale about the man and the boar is all one thing. Perhaps the truth and the tale about anything is all one thing."

"Should we do him, boss?" ask Fred and Ted.

"Aye!" snarls the boar man, opening his jaws and showing his teeth. "Aye! Do it now! But before ye do, did ye hear the tale about the man that had no tales?"

"No, sir!"

"A tale came along and gobbled him up!"

And the boar man jumps up onto his counter and opens his jaws again and roars.

FORTY-ONE

Back we go to the traffic lights at the end of the road into town. The lights are red. The traffic's at a halt. The policeman's standing there, of course, watching out for wickedness and fishiness.

A tractor pulling a cart full of hay draws up. The driver turns in his seat and calls behind him, "It's the end of the road, you two!"

The policeman hears, and he watches.

Two figures clamber down from the cart. They're stumbling, sticklike figures, like scarecrows.

"Thank you, sir!" they call to the driver. "Thank you, kind sir!"

"Think nowt of it. Glad to be of service," answers the driver.

The lights turn green; the traffic moves on.

The policeman grins. *What have we here?* he thinks as he proceeds towards the scarecrow pair with his hands behind his back. The ugly grin turns to a tender smile upon his face.

"Good evening," he says, ever so polite.

"Good evening, sir," say Annie and Ernie, for of course it is they.

"Welcome to our modest town," says the policeman. "And what might you be after in this place?"

"Oh, sir," says Ernie. "We are searching for a lost boy."

"A poor ickle lost boy?" replies the policeman.

"Yes, sir," says Annie. "He is a good boy, sir. He is this tall and he has a bonny face and there is goodness glowing from his eyes. I don't suppose you have . . .?"

"Goodness?" says the policeman. "I see many boys in the course of my work, but not too many who have *goodness* glowing from them."

"Then you would know him easily, sir," says Ernie.

The policeman ponders. He strokes his cheek, scratches his head. "No," he murmurs. "I recall a high degree of wickedness, but . . . How is it, if I may ask, that you came to *lose* him?"

Ernie looks down at the pavement. "Oh, sir," he says. "I have only myself to blame. I did not treat him right. He ran away."

"He *ran away,* and yet you tell me that he is a

good boy. Can a runaway ever be a *good* boy?"

"Oh yes, sir!" cries Annie.

"And what is more—can those who do not treat their children right be good themselves?"

"No, sir," whispers Ernie. "But I have seen the errors of my ways and I have changed."

"Too *late!*" snaps the policeman. "Your wickedness has been unleashed upon the world! We have an evil runaway in our midst. Now you follow him and think the world will be all lovey-dovey to you. IT WILL NOT! I should take you away this very minute and slap you in my darkest cell!"

"Oh, please no, sir!" begs Annie.

"What did you expect?" asks the policeman. "Did you think I would escort you to the nearest five-star hotel? Did you expect to be offered jacuzzi baths and handmade chocolates and four-poster beds?"

"Oh no, sir," says Annie. "We do not want luxuries."

"*Luxuries?* I'll give you *luxuries!*" The policeman points across the road to the narrow lane opposite. "Get out of my sight," he snarls, "before I slap the cuffs on you! Follow that lane. You'll be at home down there with the rest of the raggle-taggle lot. You'll find plenty of holes to hide in and ditches to kip in. Go a bit further and you'll even find a river to fling yourselves in." His eyes glitter in the sinking light. "If I so much as catch a *glimpse* of you two again . . ."

Annie and Ernie scuttle across the road. They dodge the traffic; they enter the potholed lane. The policeman sniggers as he watches them go. Oh, how he loves his work!

"A nasty man," says Ernie.

"Maybe he's just had a difficult day," says Annie.

She takes Ernie's arm and they stumble together through the darkness down the lane.

"You're right, dear," says Ernie. "Maybe he's just had a very difficult day."

FORTY-TWO

One by one and million by million the stars start to shine. The pale moon brightens. All across the fairground field the lights begin to flicker, flash, and glow. People scream and laugh in the cooling air, and music thuds and wails and shrieks. Many make their way in hushed excitement to a place that seems more still than any other, a place where a simple wheeled trailer stands with a tarpaulin draped across its front, bearing the simple words:

! STANLEY POTTS !

A floodlight shines upon the scene. And a spotlight makes a circle of brightness upon the blue tarpaulin, a circle that awaits the performer. The crowd gathers and grows. People eat popcorn and crisps and candyfloss. They eat sugary rock in the shape of little walking sticks and moulded into plates of English breakfast. They chew on chops and boar burgers. They swig beer and lemonade and bottles of black pop.

"Where is he?" is the whisper. "Where is Stanley Potts? Have *you* seen him yet?"

Nobody has, for Stan is in Pancho Pirelli's caravan. He's looking at the photographs of Pancho as a boy; he's looking at the great changes that came upon that boy and turned Pancho into the man he is today. He's looking further back in time, to the great Pedro Perdito. This is his ancestry. This is the line of history that leads to him, to Stanley Potts. And Stanley shakes a little, and trembles.

"Nervous, Stan?" says Pancho.

"Yes," admits the boy.

"Scared they'll eat you up? Scared it's the day of doom?"

Stan ponders, then he shakes his head. "No," he says. He trembles again, suddenly. "I'm scared of something, but I don't know what." Then he knows. "I'm just scared of doing it in front of all those folk, Mr. Pirelli." Then he knows some more. "And I'm scared of changing. I'm scared of becoming a different Stanley Potts."

Pancho smiles. "I know the feeling. As for doing it in front of all those folk, it's only natural to be nervous, and a bit of nervousness will help you to perform. As for changing? What happens is you'll not be a *completely* different Stanley Potts. You'll be the new and the old Stanley all at once. You'll be the Stan of hook-a-duck, the Stan of the days in Fish Quay Lane, *and* you'll be the brand-new Stan who swims with the piranhas. Be all those things together at once, and that's where your real greatness'll be."

Stan listens to the great Pancho Pirelli. He allows his memories to gather in his mind. He has faded visions of his time as a toddler with his mum and dad. He sees himself walking hand in hand with Uncle Ernie and Auntie Annie by the shipyards and the glittering river. He recalls the fish-canning factory and all the torments there. He remembers the goldfish, the tender thirteenth fish, and Dostoyevsky and Nitasha and the hook-a-duck. He brings them all into his mind and they flow together there. And he brings to his mind the piranha tank and the fish, and their teeth and their graceful dancing. And he realizes that his memories and his mind are astonishing things.

And he looks at Pancho Pirelli and he calmly says, "I'm ready, Mr. Pirelli. Let's go out to the tank."

FORTY-THRee

Suddenly there's Stan, stepping into the spotlight beneath his name. He wears his cape, his trunks, his goggles. He wears a look of calm determination on his face. There are gasps of excitement and delight. Children squeal.

"It's him!" the whisper goes. "It's Stanley Potts."

"*Him?*" say some. "That scrawny little feller there?"

"That *can't* be him!"

"It *is.*"

"He's too *little.*"

"It *is.*"

"He's too *scrawny.*"

"It *is!*"

"He's too *young.*"

"That *can't* be *the* Stanley Potts."

Pancho Pirelli steps into the spotlight at Stanley's side. The voices hush.

"This," says Pancho, "is Stanley Potts."

"So it is," they say.

"I told you," they say.

Pancho raises his hand and there's silence. He draws aside the tarpaulin, and there they are, swimming through the beautiful illuminated water, the awful fishy fiends, the dreadful devils with teeth like razors and jaws like traps.

"And these," says Pancho, "are my piranhas!" There are squeaks and squeals and gasps and groans.

Pancho raises his hand again. "Ladies and gentlemen," he whispers. "You are about to see something wondrous. You are about to see something that will live forever in your dreams."

More squeaks and squeals and gasps and groans.

"But first of all," says Pancho, "you must get your money out, and you must pay."

Stan stays standing in the spotlight as Pancho steps into the crowd holding out his velvet bag. Pancho murmurs his thanks as coins drop into the bag. He mutters encouragement. "Dig deeper, sir. Perhaps a little more, madam? That's better, much better. Oh, thank you, you are very kind." He voices his disappointment. "Is that *really* all you will give? You expect so

much for such a pittance?" He seeks out the reluc-
tant ones. "I can *see* you. You can't escape the eyes
of Pancho Pirelli. Money is what we need. Please
give it now."

Once or twice his voice is raised as if in anger.
*"Do you realize that a boy is about to risk his life for
your entertainment?"*

And all the time the murmurs of excitement grow.

From the back of the crowd, from the shadows
between two caravans, five pairs of eyes watch.
Five pairs of eyes that belong to five burly blokes
dressed in black.

"What's goin' to happen, boss?" asks one of the
blokes.

"Somethin' of the deepest darkest fishiness,"
says Clarence P. He points to Stan. "I should of
knowed what that monster in the spitlight would
get up to. We should of put a stop to him way back
in Fish Quay Lane."

"I can *see* you, you know," says Pancho, weaving his way through the crowd towards them.
"There's no need to hide in the dark. No need to
be shy, gentlemen."

"We is not shy!" says Clarence P. "We is

watchin' with our eyes peeled! We is the envistigators of all things fishy. And there is something fishy here!"

"Indeed there is," agrees Pancho. "There is something very, *very* fishy here."

"I knowed it!" cries Clarence P. "It is a nutter disgrace! We is here to put a stop to it!"

"Put a stop to what?" says Pancho.

"To what is going to happen!" says Clarence P.

"And what is that?" asks Pancho.

Clarence P. narrows his eyes. "Do not try to bumboozle Clarence P. Clapp, Mr. Moneybags. I knows your tricks and they will not work with me!"

Pancho smiles. He moves into the shadows, closer to Clarence P. He puts his arm round Clarence P.'s shoulder. "Do not be frightened, Mr. Clapp," he says. "Or may I call you Clarence?"

"You may not!" says Clarence P. "Unhand me, Mr. Moneybags!"

"Clarence P. Clapp is never frightened!" says Fred.

"No?" says Pancho. "Then perhaps *he* would like to enter the tank."

The lads look at Clarence P. His eyes glitter in the moonlight.

"Unhand me, I said!" he cries. "This is all ati-shoo of lies and daftness and bumboozlements."

"Is it now?" says Pancho.

"It is. That boy is a devil, and you, sir, is a slippery fish if ever I seen one."

Pancho laughs.

"And them fish there . . ." says Clarence P., pointing to the tank.

"Them fish there?" says Pancho.

". . . is not what you said they is," finishes Clarence P.

"Not piranhas?" says Pancho.

"They is not."

"Let me clarify, Clarence." Pancho points towards Stan and the fish tank. "That boy over there is one of the bravest boys you will ever see. And those fish over there are some of the fiercest fish you will ever see. And that brave boy is about to swim with those fierce fish."

Fred snorts. "That squirt?" he says. "And them tiddlers?"

"Yes," says Pancho.

"I could 'ave that squirt for me dinna and them tiddlers for me puddin'!" scoffs Ted.

"And drink the water for me soup!" adds Doug.

"Perhaps you should *try* it," Pancho tells them. "Come with me to the tank. Stick a finger in."

"Aha," says Clarence P. "Do not listen, Lads. Mr. Moneybags is trying to tempt you and lead you into fishy waters. It is all tricks and fakery. There is no rhyme nor raisin to it, and we has no wish to take part in such a spectacle, sir. Unhand me and be off. We will be watchin'. One sign of fishiness and we will be down on it like a ton of bricks."

The lads laugh and begin to gather around Pancho. "Tiny tiddlers!" they grunt. They're about to grab him, but he's gone, weaving his way once more through the crowd.

"Be strong, lads," says Clarence P. "We is in one of the world's dark, dark places. We is in the middle of the land of Rackanruwin. Watch and listen, and learn."

The lads peer at Pancho, at Stan, at the crowd, at the fish swimming sweetly in the illuminated tank.

"One day, lads," declares Clarence P., "all daftness will be drove out from the world. There'll be no daft places like this, no daft people like these around us, no daft fishy tanks and no daft fishy goings-on."

"That'll be good, boss," says Alf.

"It will," agrees Clarence P.

"So there'll just be people like us?" says Doug.

"Aye," says Fred. "People what knows what's what."

"Correct," says Ted. "Undaft people what knows what's what in a world what's got no daftness in it."

"Well said, Ted," says Clarence P. "I couldn't of put it better meself."

FORTY-FOUR

For a lad that started off with hardly any family or friends at all, our Stan's doing pretty well as he stands waiting to dive into the tank. There's Pancho, of course, weaving back and forth with the heavy velvet bag in his hand. There's Dostoyevsky and Nitasha watching nervously and proudly from the front of the crowd. There's the boar man, and the fang lady, and Tickle Peter, and Mr. Smith, and Seabrook. There's the people Stan sat by the fire with as he ate his spud, and all the kids he's met, and all the folk that have waved and grinned at him and called out his name. And there's a whole audience of other folk watching him and wishing him well.

Meanwhile, let's look back through the shadows to the potholed lane; and here they come, stumbling along hand in hand, the ones who loved him right from the start, the ones who must get here in time to see him perform: Annie and Ernie. They move towards the lights, towards the music and cries and laughter that echo in the air.

"It's a fairground, Ernie!" says Annie.

"So it is," says Ernie.

"I love a fair," says Annie. "And there was a time when you did too. Remember?"

"I remember," answers Ernie sadly, thinking of the fair that left the day Stan went away.

Annie holds his hand tighter. "Used to be lovely, didn't it?" she said. "When we were young 'uns. Spinning on the waltzer, playing hook-a-duck and winning prizes, getting our fortunes told by the gypsy."

"'You will meet a young and lovely lass!' That's what the Gypsy said to me. And I did, and it was you!"

"And she said I'd meet a tall and handsome man. And so I did, and it was you."

Ernie smiles, then sighs. "And look what I brought you to, my poor love."

"Never worry. It'll turn out right," says Annie.

"Will it?" says Ernie.

"Yes, it will," says a voice from behind them. "As long as your hearts are good and true."

They turn, and Gypsy Rose is standing there, with the moonlight shining on her and the distant fairground lights flashing behind her. "Don't worry," she says softly. "I am no danger to you."

Annie steps closer to her.

"My name is Gypsy Rose," she tells them.

"You're her!" Annie exclaims. "The Gypsy Rose I met at the fair when I was just a girl. But you can't be!"

Gypsy Rose smiles. "No, I can't possibly be," she murmurs. "Can I? It must be a trick of the moonlight. Do you have silver with which to cross my palm?"

"We've nothing but copper," says Ernie.

 He's looking closely at her as well: her face, her figure, the clothes she wears; he's listening closely to her voice. "It *is* you," he whispers. "But it *can't* be you."

Gypsy Rose smiles again. "Let us say that the moonlight is your silver." She opens her hand and lets the moonlight fall across her palm. "Thank you for it," she says. "Now, open your hands and let me look."

She reaches out and takes their open hands. She tells Annie and Ernie that moonlight is the purest and most truth-telling light. They look down together at the complicated creases and cracks and bulges there.

"Oh, you have been through difficult times," says Gypsy Rose. "Times of trouble and loss and pain." Her face falls and she groans in disappointment. She turns her eyes to Ernie's face. "Oh, Ernest!" she sighs.

"Me?" says Ernie.

"You have not always been the man you should have been."

"But he's a *good* man," says Annie.

"Is he? Can he be a good man when he has done what he has done?"

"Yes, he can!" replies Annie. "And he has seen the errors of his ways."

"Oh, has he?"

"Yes. He just turned a little bit . . . mad for a time. Didn't you, Ernie?"

Gypsy Rose watches him. "Well?" she says.

"It's true," he says. "I was led astray. I led myself astray in the search for fame and fortune."

"There's madness and there's madness," says Gypsy Rose. "There's madness that does harm, but there's also madness that does good." She stares at their open palms again. "You are searching for something. Or for someone. Am I right?"

"We had a boy," says Annie. "A boy with eyes as clear as water and a heart as bright as the moon. Will we find him, Gypsy Rose?"

"Remember him and look upon the moon," says Gypsy Rose. "The moon burns brightest when it is filled with our yearning. Stare into the moon and call out with your hearts for your lost boy."

Annie and Ernie lift their eyes and stare and yearn, and they see the moon burn brighter. And just a few hundred yards away, their boy, Stan, steps out of the spotlight for a moment. He too stares up into the moon and yearns for his lost family, and the moon burns brighter still. And for a fleeting second they all see one another there, held within the moon's bright disc, and they call out one another's names.

"Come to me!" whispers Stan. "Please come to me!"

And Annie and Ernie say to Gypsy Rose, "Where will we find him?"

But Gypsy Rose has gone, disappeared into the shadows and the darkness behind the light. So they take each other's hand and stumble onwards, hurrying towards the fair. They pass between the caravans at the edge, and slip past the sideshows, and the tent that looks like the world, and the wrestling booth, and the Wild Boar Cookhouse, and they're drawn towards the dense crowd at the heart of the fair, towards the gasps and laughter and the excited murmurings.

They arrive at the edge of the crowd; they try to peer through; they stand on tiptoe.

"What's going on?" asks Annie.

"Dunno," says Ernie. "Can't see, love."

Then they both see. There's a boy in a cloak standing before a great illuminated fish tank. He's lit by a spotlight.

"It's a boy," says Annie.

"It can't be!" gasps Ernie.

"No!"

"It *is!*"

"It *is!*"

"Stan!" they call. "STAN!"

But their voices are lost in the clamour of other voices that start to echo through the air.

"Stan! Stan! Stan! Stan!"

"What's he going to *do*?" cries Ernie.

The pair try to squirm through the people standing in front of them. "It's our boy," they keep saying. "Please let us through to our boy."

But their progress is slow. The people are packed in so tight.

"STAN! What are you going to do?"

FORTY-FiVE

"This is the moment of truth!" announces Pancho Pirelli.

The crowd quietens.

"You see before you," says Pancho, "a boy who was raised by the shores of the Orinoco."

"We see *what*?" says Ernie.

"The *Orinoco*?" says Annie.

"Will this extraordinary boy dance with the piranhas?" says Pancho.

"Will he *what*?" says Ernie.

"Or will he be gobbled up before your very eyes?"

"*WHAT?*" yells Annie.

"*WHAT?*" yells Ernie.

"*STAN!*" they yell together. "*STAN! IT'S US!*"

But the crowd is agitated again. They're muttering and shouting. They're pushing closer to the tank. Annie and Ernie still can't get through.

"That's our boy!" they cry. "Let us through to our boy!"

And others around them are saying, "He's just a

lad. He's just a skinny, scrawny little kid. How can he do a thing like this?"

"He *can't!*" say Annie and Ernie. "He's just an ordinary little lovely lad."

Inside himself, Stan isn't skinny or scrawny anymore. He's brave and strong and poised at the edge of something marvellous. He takes off his cloak. He starts to climb the ladder. The fish swim upwards. Stan pauses at the top. He lowers his goggles. He raises his hand to wave and the crowd turns silent except for a pair of horrified voices.

"STAN! STAN! WHAT ON EARTH ARE YOU DOING?"

Stan stops dead and listens. He lifts the goggles and scans the crowd. And he sees them, waving desperately at him, trying to make their way to him. They call his name again and again. His heart is filled with joy.

"Auntie Annie!" he shouts. "Uncle Ernie!"

"DON'T *DO* IT, SON!" yells Annie.

"GET DOWN, STAN!" yells Ernie.

Stan laughs. He pulls the goggles down again. "Don't worry!" he calls. "I'm doing it for you!"

"We don't *want* you to do it for us!" yells Ernie.

Stan laughs
again. "Watch!" he calls.
He spreads his arms
wide. He leaps, brings his
hands together, curves forward and down,
and makes a perfect dive into the piranha tank.

The fish part, as if they're welcoming one of
their own into the shoal. They swim downwards
with Stan as he completes his dive. They swim
upwards as he kicks himself up from the bottom
of the tank. They behave exactly as if it's Pancho
Pirelli or Pedro Perdito in the water with them.
Stan spins, and they swirl in perfect order around
him. He hangs still at the centre of the tank and
they separate into perfect groups on either side of
him. He sways and they sway. He dances and they
dance. He swims to the surface, gulps air, and
swims back down again. He gazes out through his
goggles and they gaze back at him.

O my companions, he whispers inside himself.

O our companion, he hears.

He tumbles and somersaults and twists and is at home in there with the lethal piranhas in the flood-lit water.

The people watch in wonder. They gather closer, closer. They'll see this in their dreams forevermore. And Ernie and Annie are mesmerized, their fears turning to excitement and joy.

"Look what he can *do!*" they tell each other. "That's Stan," they tell the people all around them. "That's our precious boy!"

"Oh, wouldn't his mum and dad have been proud?" breathes Annie.

Stan swims upwards and gulps air again. He swims back down again. He thinks of the thirteenth fish and the thirteenth fish's companions. He has a vision of a tin marked **Potts's Gorgeous Glittering Goldfish.** He sees the tin opening, the lid curling back, and a dozen goldfish pour out from it, in a burst of brilliant flickering gold, to swim with him and the piranhas. And as they swim there in perfect

order, the savage piranhas, the timid goldfish, and the scrawny boy, Stan looks out through the wall of the tank and sees his friends and his family, all blending into one: Dostoyevsky and Nitasha, Pancho Pirelli, Auntie Annie and Uncle Ernie.

And he sees for a fleeting moment, closest of all to the tank, his mum and dad. They smile and wave at him and mouth, *We're so proud of you, Stan. We love you, Stan.*

And then they're gone.

Stan swims up to the surface. He grips the ladder. He climbs out. He stands there and bows. The crowd roars and roars. And then Stan climbs back down and rushes into the arms of Annie and Ernie Potts.

FORTY-SIX

So let's say hurrah for Stanley Potts. He's a boy that's become a different kind of boy. He's the scrawny kid who grew up with all kinds of trouble, fishiness and daftness, but who's brave and bold enough to be the hero of this tale. His life has opened up before him. He'll swim with piranhas night after night. He won't get eaten. Piranhas aren't really that dangerous after all—or not if we are to believe Pancho Pirelli. Maybe in a while Stan'll leave the piranhas behind, find other challenges to face. Maybe he will go to the Amazon and the Orinoco. Maybe he'll go to Siberia and Ashby de la Zouch. Certainly he'll keep on finding other ways to grow, and he'll become an even different kind of Stanley Potts.

And his family, which has become such a different kind of family, will grow and change along with him. There they all are, celebrating together happily, with the cheering crowd around them. Pancho draws the tarpaulin back across the tank. Now they'll all head towards the hook-a-duck, where they'll light a fire, nibble scorching spuds, and drink black pop. Let's let them go. Let's leave them to their celebrations and their memories, and their plans for splendid futures.

The crowd disperses. The lights start to dim. The moon drops towards the horizon and the endless stars in the endless darkness glitter and glow. Every heart beats faster. Every eye is shining. Every mind contains the seeds of weird and wonderful dreams. Even Tickle Peter, after all his years of glumness, smiles.

Oh, and here they come, out of the shadows, moving into the spaces left behind by the happy ones: Clarence P. Clapp and his daft lads, Doug and Alf and Fred and Ted. Look, they're sneaking towards the fish tank. Could it be that Clarence P. is about to prove that they aren't piranhas after all? They're getting closer. They're lifting the tarpaulin. They're laughing at the tiny tiddlers. They're jeering and mocking, as daft lads do. Oh, and look. Clarence P. is already on the ladder. He's climbing up. Surely he's not going to jump into the . . .

What do *you* think should happen? Should Clarence P. jump in? Maybe it doesn't matter if he does. Maybe the piranhas will prove to be tiny tiddlers after all. But maybe Clarence P. *should* get gobbled up. After all, Clarence P. and Doug and Alf and Fred and Ted aren't exactly angels, are they? They've done some pretty nasty stuff in this story. Look what they did to Annie and Ernie. Imagine what they did to that poor motorist. Imagine the bother they're going to cause in the future. And Clarence P., who's nearly at the top of the ladder now, is the boss. Some would say, of course, that blokes like Clarence P. and the daft lads are just misled. Maybe they had troubled childhoods. Maybe there are a few important cells missing from their brains. Maybe they need some counselling, or to have some music played to them, or somebody just to give them a good cuddle. I can't decide.

Anyway, Clarence looks down at the piranhas. He looks down at the lads.

"Jump in, boss," says Doug.

"These is just tiddlers," says Alf.

"Jump," says Fred.

"Well said, Fred," says Ted.

Clarence P. is now at the edge.

It's up to you. If you were writing the story, what would *you* make happen? Does he jump? And if he jumps, what happens next? Maybe it'll help to think about what Stanley Potts, the hero of our story, might make Clarence P. do. Or maybe it doesn't really matter at all. Whatever you decide, this is just a story. Clarence P. Clapp only exists in the pages of this book and in that mysterious place, your imagination.

Anyway, decide now if you'd like to. Then there's one last little chapter to bring us to the end.

FORTY-SEVEN

Of course, there's never really a proper end. The people who've lived through this tale will live through many more. But we have to come to a halt somewhere, and this is it. Let's rise and fly. Let's leave behind the fairground field and everybody in it. Let's go higher, higher. The field with its lights and noise diminishes. We see the town spread out beyond it, and the strings of lights linking this to other glowing towns and cities. We see the darkness of the silent countryside, the gleaming tracks of meandering rivers. We see the deep dark sea. We go higher and see the galaxies of cities scattered across the world. We see the great tracts of wilderness. We see the oceans and the snow-capped peaks of mountains.

And oh, we go so high we see the whole world itself. Just look at that great and gorgeous sphere of light and dark. See how it turns, how day gives way to night and night to day. See how the seas shine blue beneath the sun and glow darkly beneath the moon. Imagine the people and the stories that can be found upon that sphere. Imagine the lives and the deaths and the loves and the dreams and the troubles and the heroes and the villains that exist down there. Imagine the story after story after story that can be found and told. Let's go even higher, so that even our great world diminishes, becomes just one world among many, many others spinning in the endless dark. How many stories now, in all this endlessness?

But let's return for one last glance. Down we go. The earth and its geography comes back into clear view. Where shall we go? Look. It's morning in Siberia. The sun gleams on the snow. There's ice on the rivers, and smoke rises from the chimneys of houses and villages spread out across the steppe. Here's a great city by a river, the city of Novosibirsk. Go closer. The air's bright and clear, and it's bitterly cold. There's the broad River Ob. Look at the skyscrapers. And the huge railway station painted pale green. There's a mighty arch as an entrance.

Let's go inside. How busy it is in here. People milling about. Trains waiting at platforms. There's a bunch of slender women heading towards one. They wear thick coats, fur hats. Their breath condenses in the bitter air. They're laughing. See that face, that figure? She looks familiar. We've seen her in a photograph, I believe. Yes, she does look lovely. Is it Nitasha's mother? Is it Mrs. Dostoyevsky? She's laughing, chatting. She's talking of home, of going home again. She jumps aboard, and the others follow, and soon the train pulls out of the station.

Maybe she is going home. Maybe there's a little more joy heading the way of Stanley Potts and his pals in their distant fairground. Let's hope so. They deserve it. After all, the hearts of these people, despite all their troubles and all their faults and failings, are good and true.

The END

From the imaginations of DAVID ALMOND
and POLLY DUNBAR *comes a story of the*
Great Human Bird Competition . . .

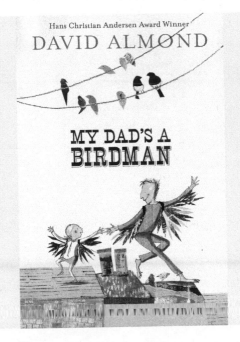

Hans Christian Andersen Award Winner
DAVID ALMOND

MY DAD'S A
BIRDMAN

Dad is building a pair of wings and eating flies.
Auntie Doreen is making far too many dumplings.
Mr. Poop is shouting louder and louder, and even
Mr. Mint, the headmaster, is getting in a flap.

"A comedic celebration of resilience." — *Chicago Tribune*

Available in hardcover, paperback, and audio

www.candlewick.com

Another delightfully outrageous expedition from

DAVID ALMOND *and* POLLY DUNBAR

In Paul's apartment building are Mabel, who calls herself Molly, and her brother, who hides under a paper bag. Then there's Clarence, a poodle who thinks he can fly. And Paul himself believes the moon is a great hole in the sky.

> ★ "Fast-paced and satisfying. Madmen are heroes and crackpots are geniuses in this charmingly over-the-top read-aloud. . . . Dunbar's abundant full-color illustrations perfectly capture the beautiful barminess of it all." —*Kirkus Reviews* (starred review)

Available in hardcover and audio

www.candlewick.com

A breathtakingly eerie graphic tale from

DAVID ALMOND *and* DAVE McKEAN

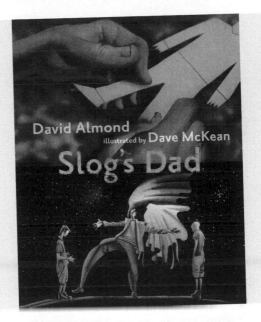

Slog believes in life after death. He believes that the scruffy man on a bench outside Myer's butcher shop is his dad, returned to visit him one last time. Slog's friend Davie isn't so sure.

★ "A haunting and beautiful book. . . . Richly and poetically illustrated." —*Publishers Weekly* (starred review)

Available in hardcover

www.candlewick.com

An original creation tale conjured by

DAVID ALMOND *and* DAVE McKEAN

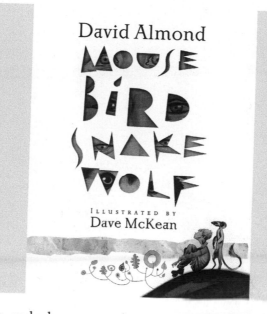

The gods have created a world with mountains, forests, and seas, people and beasts, but there are curious gaps in it. Harry, Sue, and Little Ben set out to fill the gaps . . .

★ "You could say that this is Almond and McKean's most beautiful effort yet, but just know that *beautiful* has its own dark and wondrous meaning in their hands." —*Booklist* (starred review)

Available in hardcover